Randa Abdel-Fattah is a twenty-seven-year-old lawyer. *Ten Things I Hate About Me* is her second novel. *Does My Head Look Big In This?* was her first, and received much critical acclaim when it was published in 2006. It won the Australian Book of the Year for Older Children in the same year.

Randa grew up in Melbourne, but now lives in Sydney. She is actively involved in the Palestinian and Muslim communities in Australia and a long-time advocate of a free Palestine. She loves travelling to Egypt and being spoilt by relatives. She also loves reading, watching romantic comedies, her husband's sense of humour, getting a seat on the train, and any movie starring Colin Firth. Randa has a baby daughter.

Praise for *Does My Head Look Big In This?*

"It's funny, it's foolish, it's serious, it takes up real issues, it tells a story and it strikes a chord. What more can you want of any book?"
Books for Keeps

"Sharp, funny and moving"
TES

"A smart, lively, contemporary story that manages to blast prejudices without feeling ponderous or worthy, with its sympathetic teenage protagonist who decides to wear the hijab full time. Every teenager in Britain should read it, so all the non-Muslims can get past being squeamish about difference and root for each other"
Sunday Times

"Packed with humour"
Glasgow Herald

"This is an eye-opening book because it articulates a Muslim teenager's struggle with misconceptions about her beliefs and her frustration at being associated with politics and media headlines while remaining funny and positive. . . It's a book about defiance, determination, intelligence and self-respect"
Telegraph

Ten Things I Hate About Me

Randa Abdel-Fattah

MARION LLOYD BOOKS

First published in the UK in 2007 by
Marion Lloyd Books
An imprint of Scholastic Ltd
Euston House, 24 Eversholt Street
London, NW1 1DB, UK

Registered office: Westfield Road, Southam, Warwickshire, CV47 0RA
SCHOLASTIC and associated logos are trademarks and or registered trademarks
of Scholastic Inc.

Copyright © Randa Abdel-Fattah, 2006
First published in Australia by Pan Macmillan Australia Pty Ltd, 2006

The right of Randa Abdel-Fattah to be identified as the author of this work has
been asserted by her.

10 digit ISBN 0 439 94371 X
13 digit ISBN 978 0439 94371 0

A CIP catalogue record for this book is available from the British Library.

Typeset by M Rules
Printed in the UK by CPI Bookmarque, Croydon, CR0 4TD

Papers used by Scholastic Children's Books are made from wood grown in
sustainable forests.

5 7 9 10 8 6 4

This is a work of fiction. Names, characters, places, incidents and dialogues are
products of the author's imagination or are used fictitiously. Any resemblance to
actual people, living or dead, events or locales is entirely coincidental.

www.scholastic.co.uk/zone

To Deyana, who kicked away in my stomach when I wrote the first draft and lay in a rocker under my computer desk when I wrote the second.

ACKNOWLEDGEMENTS

Thank you to the team at Scholastic for all your wonderful efforts in publishing and promoting my books. Special thanks to Marion Lloyd. It is both a delight and honour to work with you. My books are truly in special hands. To my agent, Sheila Drummond: thank you for your friendship, expertise, wisdom and inspiring pep talks.

Juggling a newborn baby with a deadline to deliver the second draft of this book was quite a challenge. I would not have been able to meet my deadline without the support of many people. My biggest thanks go to Tant Thanna, who selflessly offered me so much of her time and support.

Thank you to my parents and sister. Your unending faith and support keeps megoing!

Finally, thankyou to my husband, Ibrahim, for his patience and love.

1

Amy, Liz and I are reminiscing about our holidays as we wait for Mr Anderson to arrive for home-room on Monday morning. The summer break is still fresh in our minds and we're slowly coming to terms with the fact that another school year has begun.

The three of us are lamenting that we can no longer wake up at noon or play video games and watch DVDs until four in the morning, when we overhear Ahmed Latif talking to Danielle Pogorni and Paul Xiang.

"Yeah, they got me with a beer bottle!" Ahmed says. "I've earned a pretty decent scar, hey?" He touches it with pride. "I look like a tough dude, don't I?"

Danielle stares at the scar in awe, reaching out to touch it.

"So what happened?" Paul asks.

Ahmed leans in close to them and, in a hushed tone, says: "The riots."

"Which riots?" Paul asks with a goofy smile. "The Christmas stocktake ones?"

"Yeah, man," Ahmed responds in a wry tone. "I got hit by a beer bottle at a riot over half-priced socks. I was talking about the *beach* riots. I was with my cousins and some of my mates. We were walking down the esplanade. We heard a crowd of people chanting. They're chanting out stuff like, *No more Lebs!*, *Wogs Go Home*, *Ethnic Cleansing*. And there were older people in the crowd too! It wasn't just kids."

At this point Amy swings back on her chair and turns her face towards Ahmed. "So how did you get attacked?" she asks.

He turns to us, surprised that he has an audience. He pauses before answering. "Well . . . I'm known to have a big mouth."

"Won't argue you with you there, mate," Paul jokes, slapping him on the shoulder.

"We walked up to some of them and started yelling stuff back."

"You're a hero," Danielle says good-naturedly. "Didn't you know that things were turning violent?"

"Nah, not then. I lost my cool. I was shouting at them, calling them racists. This old guy was yelling out that his dad fought in the war and he was a fair-dinkum Aussie and that we should go back to our desert caves!"

2

"He had a point," Chris Ross says, sniggering. "Why don't you?"

"We're currently renovating our cave," Ahmed snaps. "All that desert sand damaged the upholstery."

Chris shoots Ahmed a nasty sneer but Ahmed ignores him and turns back to Danielle and Paul. "All of a sudden my mates and I were surrounded. Most of the skips were off their faces with alcohol. But they knew what they were doing. Anyway, I got struck by a bottle. I didn't even see it coming. It hurt like hell! Man, I was angrier than a constipated giraffe."

"Well, you kind of brought it on yourself," Liz says. "I mean, *you* walked up to them." She glances at me for support but I pretend to be fascinated by an ingrown fingernail.

"*Excuse me?* They were calling us wogs. Giving us shit for being Lebanese. They were telling us to get off *their* turf. Do you think we're going to sit back and take it? I've been going to that beach since I was a kid. It's mine just as much as theirs."

Peter Clarkson, the most popular guy in my year, suddenly joins the conversation. "Man, you ethnics and Asians are always complaining." For reasons only apparent to him he suddenly assumes the voice of a pitiful heroine in a nineteenth century novel. "*Oh help me! I'm a victim of racism. The white people are out to get me.* Get over yourselves!"

Chris bursts out laughing.

3

"You ethnics and Asians?" Paul murmurs to himself in a tone of disbelief. "Who says that any more?"

"Don't call us ethnics. We're *Aussies*," Ahmed says furiously.

"Oh come on! Even our politicians have singled your kind out as troublemakers," Sam Richards says. "You just refuse to integrate. Your women wear that funny headgear and most of you don't speak English." He looks sheepishly at Danielle who is sending him death stares. "You're Italian, you're OK. You brought us pizza!"

"Oh thank you so much, Sam," Danielle says. "I feel honoured to be *accepted* by you. Why don't you piss off and skull a beer? You know, do something in line with your genetics."

Sam sneers at her and Peter sits up tall in his chair and coolly looks Ahmed and Danielle up and down. "I agree with Sam. If you want to be Aussie you have to abandon your culture. And if you're so oppressed by this country, you can always go back to where you came from."

"You mean, Guildford," Paul asks hotly. "Postcode Sydney 2161?"

Ahmed, Danielle and Paul give Peter, Chris and Sam disgusted looks and turn their backs on them.

Peter, who is sitting at the desk next to mine, leans across and smiles conspiratorially at me. "The delusions of immigrants," he whispers, and smirks.

I smile back meekly. That's what I do when I interact with Peter. I do coy, self-conscious, shy. That is the extent of my repertoire.

4

I deliberately drop my pen on the floor, leaning down to grab it so that he can't see the red flush creeping over my face. When I'm sure that I've regained my normal pigmentation I raise my head.

Peter leans over again and says: "What a joke, hey Jamie? Ahmed probably spends his weekends in a garage making bombs or training for a terrorist cell. I'm glad the riots broke out. My dad told me that it's been a long time coming. He used to surf those beaches when he was younger. Sure, there were Italians and Greeks but there weren't *too* many, so you didn't notice and it was OK. But now the Lebs have invaded the beaches and it's not the same."

I gulp hard and nod half-heartedly, trying to disguise my mortification at his comments.

You see, neither Peter nor anybody else in my class has any idea about my Lebanese-Muslim background. In fact, my real name is Jamilah Towfeek but I'm known as Jamie when I'm at school because I'm on a mission to de-wog myself.

I attend Guildford High, a run-down, underfunded public school in Sydney's west. We only have the facilities to make cup-a-soup for home economics, and rumour has it that our lockers were purchased at a garage sale held by the local prison.

In my school there is clear division between ethnics, skips, nerds and loners. I don't mean to say that it's gang warfare or anything like that. In fact, there has only been one alleged incident of racist violence, involving a nail file, a plate of Asian greens and a bowl of miso soup.

5

The kids of Anglo-Saxon background are called "skips". Anybody from the Middle East or Mediterranean is an "ethnic" or a "wog". Samoans and New Zealanders are "FOB"s (Fresh Off The Boat). There's also the "Asian" crowd, which makes no distinction between Chinese, Japanese, Malaysian or any of the other 4 billion people who happen to come from the largest continent on earth. Computer geeks, sci-fi addicts, acne-riddled individuals, anyone wearing bifocal lenses and loners are in a category all of their own.

Ever since Year Seven (I'm in Year Ten now), I've hidden the fact that I'm of Lebanese-Muslim heritage to everybody at school to avoid people assuming I drive planes into buildings as a hobby.

Peter leads the cool skip group. He doesn't walk into class, he glides, collecting the adulation of people around him as he passes. If life was a movie his eyes would twinkle every time he talked and he'd always be minty fresh. He laps up attention like a puppy at a bowl of water. He entertains: burps songs, spins a tennis ball in class, drives supply teachers to nervous breakdowns. He can be a bully but most of us laugh at his performances as a protective measure. Oh, and most importantly, according to Peter, non-Anglos aren't real Aussies. They're imposters. Fraudulent Australians.

Being seen with Peter is a one-way ticket to coolness. Being liked by Peter is the stuff of dreams.

Unlike Danielle and Ahmed, I don't have the courage to be upfront about who I am. I'd rather not deal with people wondering if I keep a picture of Osama Bin Laden in the shape of a love heart under my pillow. Call me crazy but I'm also not particularly excited about the prospect of having to stand accused every time somebody who happens to be of Lebanese background commits a crime.

So I've anglicized my name. And dyed my hair blonde. And I sometimes wear blue contact lenses. Maybe the logic isn't apparent. But when you have brown hair and brown eyes, avoiding a "Middle Eastern appearance" tag at my school is made easier when you're hiding behind peroxide and optical aids.

When I walked into the lounge room as a blonde my dad glanced at me, choked on his coffee and started praying aloud to Allah to give him patience. Allah must have been listening because I managed to convince him that the sudden change in my hair colour would not mean I'd end up nightclubbing or on the arm of a boyfriend.

The blonde locks have probably helped me in my mission to stay incognito. Nobody at school knows about my background. I'm not popular enough for people to want to probe, and I'm not loser enough for people to think my vagueness is weird. I guess you could say that I don't make much of an impact. That's why when Peter started talking to me in home-room this morning I soaked up his attention like a biscuit dipped in coffee. The fact that his comments have left me soggy and wilted doesn't matter. That's the price you pay when you withdraw to the safety of anonymity.

*

7

"Do you think Ahmed was overreacting?" Amy asks Liz and me as we walk to class.

"No way," I say. "Of course he'd be angry. He was attacked."

"Sam had a point, though," Liz says. "Don't you think?"

Amy shrugs. "I'm not sure I agree with him. I mean, nobody gives Italians a hard time for raising their flags for Italy when the soccer is on or for speaking Italian."

"Who cares anyway," Liz says flippantly. "It doesn't affect us."

That's what she thinks.

"I like Sam," Liz says.

"I figured." Amy rolls her eyes. "That was the main topic of conversation all holidays. Every time we went out I had to put up with you replaying your telephone conversations with him." Noticing my blank expression, she tells Liz to fill me in.

Liz turns to me and grins. "He asked for my number on the last day of school and we've been in contact throughout the holidays. Remember that time we went to Westfield Parramatta, Amy? We counted fifty-three text messages in the space of three hours!"

"Don't remind me," Amy groans.

"Or the time you slept over at my place and I made you pause the movie every ten minutes because he kept calling."

Amy shakes her head and gives Liz a disgusted look.

Although Amy and Liz are my friends, they're closer to each other and basically tolerate me as something of a third wheel. Whereas Amy and Liz spend hours on the phone and go out on weekends, I rarely see them outside of school. There's a definite distance between us, and I have to say that it's deliberate on my part.

I avoid getting too close to Amy or Liz, or anyone else at school for that matter. If I get too close then I run the risk of exposing myself. And I am determined that nobody, not even Amy or Liz, ever gains the slightest clue as to my background and what my family life is like.

Amy and Liz seem to have it all. They're untouched by stereotypes, racism and family problems. They're of Anglo background. They have blonde hair and blue eyes. They don't have a strict curfew and never seem to have a problem getting permission to go out on the weekend.

I envy them. Sometimes the Jamie in me aches to be a blue-eyed, blonde girl of Caucasian appearance. The yard-stick against which all Australians are measured.

The Jamilah in me longs to be respected for who she is, not tolerated and put up with like some bad odour or annoying house guest. But it takes guts to command that respect and deal with people's judgements. Being Jamie at school shelters me from confronting all that.

"Sam's a great guy," Liz says. "Don't you think, Jamie?"

"To be honest, he scares me," I say. "That whole group does."

"Why?" Amy asks.

"I feel like I have to pass a popularity test to talk to them."

"Peter was talking to you back in home-room," Liz says. "So you can't be doing too badly."

"That was a one-off. He usually doesn't look twice at me."

We enter the science lab and Sam bounces over.

"Hey Liz, want to be my partner today? We're dissecting frogs."

Liz grins, nods enthusiastically and walks over to Sam's benchtop.

"So I guess that leaves you and me as partners then," Amy says.

A wave of relief floods through me. Because Amy and Liz have always been Siamese twins at school, I've always dreaded classes where we have to pair up, as I'm inevitably left looking for someone to join me.

Amy and I walk over to a benchtop and start preparing for our dissection assignment. As we're arranging the equipment I notice Timothy Reynolds leaning against a desk. His arms are folded across his chest, legs lazily stretched out as he surveys the class, seemingly oblivious to the fact that he needs to find a lab partner.

Just then Mr Govan turns his back from the blackboard and, noticing Timothy, snaps: "This isn't a cafeteria, Timothy. Find a partner and start your work."

"I haven't got a partner," Timothy says in a casual tone.

I'm struck by his quiet confidence. He's admitted to the entire class that he's a loner and it doesn't seem to have bothered him.

Then again, Timothy's never been a conformist. He started at Guildford High midway through the last term of last year. He used to live on the North Shore, the affluent side of

Sydney. His parents divorced and he moved over to this end of town to live with his mother. Most kids would loathe spending recess or lunch time alone or not having somebody to sit next to in class. It's bad for the image. But he's the type who seems to have no problem spending time by himself. He doesn't discriminate about who he hangs out with either. At school there are certain groups that you wouldn't dare to be associated with because of the impact on your reputation. For example, the computer geeks, who are known to do little else at lunch time than sit around eating home-made cheese and tomato sandwiches, talking about java scripts and popping their pimples. Timothy, however, has no problem going up to them, slapping a handshake and discussing hard drives and software.

Maybe people feel intimidated by his "don't give a stuff what people think" attitude. But I, for one, am in awe that somebody can be so confident in themselves that they don't care who they hang out with or what people whisper behind their back.

And boy are there whispers. I reckon there are different levels of bullying. Timothy doesn't get beaten up or shoved around. He cops the verbal bullying. Personally, I'd prefer physical assault. One punch and you're down. But persistent name-calling? That prolongs the hurt. It stretches it out. Each nasty word stretches the rubber band further away until finally, one day, it snaps back at you with maximum impact.

Of course, it doesn't help that Timothy's intelligent. Or

that he's not into sport, which seems to be a prerequisite for male coolness at my school. In his first week he mentioned that he liked tropical fish and came into class with *An Almanac of Tropical Fish*, yellow Post-it notes jutting out of its pages. Peter and his group immediately nicknamed Timothy "Goldfish" and ever since then the name has stuck.

The thing about Timothy is that he seems to handle it well. There have been no reports of counselling sessions with our school psychologist or any Dear Diary incidents. He usually hits back with a sarcastic remark and moves on. Perhaps some of the guys think he can take it and that's why they keep on giving him a hard time. I just keep on thinking of that elastic band stretching and stretching.

"Is there anybody else who doesn't have a partner?" Mr Govan asks the class.

I glance over at Peter who's sniggering with his friends.

Carlos slowly raises his hand and Mr Govan tells him to join Timothy. Carlos shuffles over, and Peter cries out, "Losers!" Carlos sticks his finger up at him but his face is flushed with self-consciousness. Timothy, on the other hand, seems unperturbed. As I watch him ignoring Peter's taunts, our eyes meet and, to my surprise, he smiles.

Amy nudges me in the side, looking over at Timothy and giggling. "What's with the eye contact?"

"No big deal."

"Do you two have something going on?"

"Get over it, will you? It was a casual smile. His facial muscles twitch and you think he's proposed to me."

She laughs. "Just checking!"

It's not that Amy's a cruel person. She doesn't tease Timothy like Peter and the other guys do. Like me, she's an onlooker. We buy tickets as audience members only. We never volunteer for the show itself. I know that's not an excuse. In fact, maybe we're worse.

Our status in the regular crowd is parasitical. It feeds off the uncoolness of others. We can only be semipopular as a measure of those who aren't. So we naturally try to maintain the status quo; support the system that supports ours. Our complicity is self-serving.

2

"**G**eorge is having a big bash at his house this weekend," Amy tells Liz and me as we walk to our lockers. "And the best part is that his cousin just turned eighteen. You know what that means?"

Everybody's going to get the chance to lean over a toilet bowl, tongue a stranger, lick Venetian blinds and give somebody an atomic wedgie.

I pretend to look enthusiastic. There is no way my dad will let me go.

"Sam asked me to go with him," Liz says excitedly.

"So that's what you two were whispering about in science," Amy says. "Are you a couple now?"

"Well he hasn't officially asked me to be his girlfriend. . ."

"Is he picking you up or are we going together, like we usually do?"

Liz looks at Amy with a guilty expression on her face. "Um . . . he's going to come by and pick me up with his older brother, who drives. I hope you don't mind. . ."

"Not a problem," Amy says in a voice which clearly indicates that it is. She suddenly starts looking for something in her bag and avoids Liz's gaze.

"Maybe you and Jamie could go together," Liz suggests.

Amy slowly looks up from her bag at me.

"Do you want to go?"

"Yeah! Sure! It should be heaps of fun!" I make sure to exaggerate my enthusiasm. That way, when I cancel at the last minute due to a sudden case of gastro — actually, I'll make it family commitments this time — she won't be suspicious. So far I've managed to keep everybody in the dark about the fact that my dad's rules make the Jurassic era seem progressive. It's too embarrassing. I'm a pro at inventing plausible excuses for last-minute cancellations.

"Great! That's settled then!" Liz says happily. "I've got to go now. I'm meeting Sam."

Her eyes go misty when she mentions his name and I can practically see the hair on her arms plait themselves into little love hearts. She dashes off just as Peter and Chris walk up to us, bouncing a basketball between them.

I try to maintain my composure. Peter always makes me nervous. All that popularity and misdirected ego.

"Are you coming to George's party on Saturday?" Peter asks us. He casts his eyes over my body. From fake blonde tip to school shoes toe. He checks me out like a customer at a butcher's sizing up the quality of a piece of meat.

"Yep," Amy answers.

"What about you, Jamie?"

"I wouldn't miss it!" I gush. I have that fake enthusiasm thing going on again.

"Then I'll definitely be going," Peter says, leaning close and flashing me a playful smile.

Excuse me? Ad break. Intermission. Something very strange is happening. Peter is flirting with *me*. My bra size hasn't increased over the holidays. I haven't had any collagen injections. And as far as I know my family is still in the lower socio-economic bracket.

I respond with a goofy smile. As you do when the most popular guy in class is blatantly flirting with you.

I try to ignore Amy's bewildered look and concentrate on being calm.

"My dad's pissed off with me," Chris says. "I ran over his fishing rod with my skateboard. He's threatened to ground me this weekend."

He says it without a hint of shame or embarrassment. I stare at him open-mouthed.

Noticing my expression, Chris grins at me. "Yeah, my dad's pretty tough."

I don't think anybody needs to know that if my dad busted me at a party with boys and drink he'd throw me into a tank with a semitranquillized shark and ask me to reflect on my actions.

"Tough!" Peter exclaims good-naturedly. "Mate, your dad's got you in chains. Remember how he busted us drinking at your place? We copped it hard! He made us clean out the garage, mow the lawn *and* do the edging."

"That's harsh," Amy says, demonstrating to me how utterly ignorant she is of the meaning of the word. "So how will you come to the party?"

"Yeah," Peter adds. "Don't be a loser. Just come. What are you going to tell everybody? Oh, sorry, guys, I can't make it because my dad won't let me? Mate, they'll roast you alive if you pull that one on them!"

I pretend to find the whole conversation amusing and join in their laughter.

"He'll get over it," Chris says, shrugging his shoulders. "And even if he doesn't, he's going to the footy on Saturday night so he won't know the difference anyway."

"Come on, let's go shoot some hoops," Peter says. He turns away and then stops and looks back at me. "I'll see you on the dance floor." He winks at me and walks away.

"What the. . .?" Amy says, in a tone that indicates that she is as baffled as I am.

"I wasn't imagining it, was I?"

"No!"

"Do you think it's a case of mistaken identity?"

We throw ourselves into a game of speculation. It's not a low self-esteem thing. I've attracted guys before. Blonde hair (I mean peroxide), piercing blue eyes (I mean contact lenses). I've had my share of wolf whistles. But the fact is, the situation lacks logic. Peter has status. That's why his dating is strategic. He will either maintain the status quo or upgrade. Tara Hanson, captain of the Year Eleven netball team, was an upgrade. Legs to her neck, boobs that defy gravity. She's loud and assertive and makes a point of being noticed. She wore the pants in the relationship, although, based on schoolyard gossip, wearing clothes didn't really feature all that much in their partnership.

I represent a downgrade. That's a simple, indisputable fact. So unless Peter's knocked his head on concrete, it doesn't make sense.

"So what will you wear?" Amy asks me.

"I'm not sure yet. I'll have to see what I can put together."

There's a moment's uncomfortable pause. Parties and weekends and what-to-wear conversations are usually Amy and Liz's domain. At first they would ask me to go out with them but they eventually gave up after one too many "I've got something else on" excuses. I've never had the courage to tell them that my dad has a policy about going out at night. It's called Never. Subtitles: Not In A Trillion Years.

"How about I come over to your place and we can get ready together?" Amy asks.

Her question zooms into my brain. There is no way I can handle Amy visiting. My background oozes out of every corner of the house. From the paintings with inscriptions from the Koran hanging on the walls, to the Lebanese satellite channel. I once heard Peter and his gang laughing about "ethnic" homes always having veggie patches in the backyard, a plastic outdoor table setting on the front verandah and a stripped Ford Falcon sitting on four bricks in the front yard. My face burned with shame that day. My dad grows cucumbers, zucchinis and tomatoes. Our table setting is bottle green. And Bilal has *two* stripped cars sitting in our car port.

I have to protect myself. My brain hits the panic button and offers me three options:

1. We're renovating and most of the power points are out, so we can't plug in our hair straighteners.
2. My sister is studying for an exam and goes feral at the slightest bit of noise.
3. My dad is having visitors over.

I opt for the power points excuse. I'm in an emergency situation here. Besides, the prospect of not being able to straighten our hair almost makes Amy shudder with fear.

"Come over to my place then?" Amy asks, giving me an awkward smile.

"OK, cool, that would be nice."

It's deceitful. It's dishonest. It's two-faced. It's all those things, yes.

But most of all, it's about survival.

I practise my speech on the way home in the bus. Deep down, though, I know it's of no use. I'm not allowed to go to the movies with my friends at night. I have more chance of waking up a natural blonde than convincing my father to let me go to George's party.

My mother died of a sudden heart attack when I was nine years old. My father changed instantly. Before my mother's death, he was fun and carefree. Afterwards, he became rigid, overprotective and paranoid. He worries about what happens and what *could* happen. He wants to control every variable in my life and it drives me mad.

Last year he drafted his curfew rules. He made me type them and hang them on the fridge door.

While I'm stuck with these Stone Age rules, my brother Bilal is allowed a lot more freedom. We're only about two years apart but he has a curfew of midnight (which he never obeys). I'm doomed to have the social life of a hibernating bear with the kind of shackles I'm in at the moment.

My dad doesn't really control my older sister, Shereen. She's twenty-two. If she's out late at night he knows she's not dancing her heels off at a nightclub or flirting with a spunky guy. She's either writing a manifesto on women's rights, working out a strategy to reduce greenhouse gas emissions, or attending a Muslim youth function, getting high on spirituality and charity events. It annoys him but she doesn't have any curfew restrictions because she's usually home early anyway.

CHARTER OF CURFEW RIGHTS FOR
JAMILAH TOWFEEK

1. Jamilah is not allowed to go out after dark. She must be home before sunset.
2. Jamilah may go to the movies with her FEMALE

20

friends *sometimes*, provided that her brother or sister or family member picks her up from the cinema immediately after the movie finishes. No loitering around in the car park permitted.

3. The movie must be in the daytime.
4. Bilal's friends do not constitute family members.
5. Under no circumstances are boys allowed.
6. Under no circumstances are boys allowed.
7. There will be NO going out until all homework is finished.

Signatories: *Dad*　　　　　　　　*Jamilah (Coerced)*
Witness: *Shereen*

I arrive home after school and enter a family war zone. Shereen and my father are arguing in the lounge room. Bilal is sprawled on the couch reading a car magazine.

"What's wrong this time?" I ask, throwing my school bag on the floor and slumping down into an armchair. I'm annoyed because I'll have to wait until my dad is in a good mood before approaching him about the party.

"Your sister is disgracing us again!" my father cries in Arabic. My father always speaks to us in Arabic.

"Since when is sticking up for what you believe in a disgrace?" she cries, hands on her hips, nostrils flaring as she faces my father.

"I'm watching the news and what do I see? My daughter in front of the camera, screaming about race riots and waving

21

her arms around like somebody has plugged an electrical cable into her ear!"

"I'm sticking up for us, Dad! Don't you get it? Social apathy and the failure to commit to open political discourse threaten the viability of our democracy!" That's how Shereen talks. As though she's memorized her class notes. We generally need a dictionary to make sense of her.

I steal a look at Bilal and we roll our eyes. We've become accustomed to Shereen and Dad arguing. My dad thinks Shereen is going to end up with an ASBO because she's constantly organizing protests and sitting on the steps of Parliament House with her hippie friends who don't understand that not wearing deodorant breaches United Nations conventions.

"The sooner our community and wider society refrains from radicalizing human-rights activism, the sooner the human race will come to terms with its common humanity and free itself of the bonds of muted rage!"

Bilal and I pretend to stick our fingers down our throats. Shereen darts a menacing look at us and my dad throws his hands in the air in frustration. "When will you abandon all these protests and just settle down and focus on your studies? These protests achieve nothing! Why do you insist on drawing attention to yourself? We live in tense times, Shereen. You already stand out as it is."

My dad's referring to the fact that Shereen wears the hijab. Last year she made the decision to ditch her purple dreadlocks for the veil. My dad was overjoyed at the time. He thought that Shereen had finally settled down.

He was wrong.

She bought bags of material and assorted patchwork. She designed a whole variety of different patterns to sew on to her veils. She has one veil with Yin Yang patches sewn all over it. She bought an embroidery kit and sewed the words *Make Peace Not War* on another veil. Other statements she's adopted are:

Save the Forests.

More Bikes, Less Cars.

Why are there never enough red jellybeans?

Vote Chocolate into the Senate.

My personal favourite is: *Don't Go Burning Your Retina On My Account.*

Needless to say, Shereen has no intention of settling down. She's as passionate and active as ever, living to save the world through protests, sit-ins, vigils and stand-offs. I sometimes think she'd have a sit-in to protest against cats being fed home-brand instead of Whiskers. It's no surprise, therefore, that she's unimpressed with my dad's desire for her to spend her weekends studying or learning a new recipe.

"I want to make a difference, Dad. And I don't see how wearing the hijab should stop me."

Bilal throws his magazine aside and groans. "Shereen, can't you just act normal for once? You seriously need to take a chill pill. You need a night at Cave. Some R&B, a little soul and funk, a Bacardi breezer and you'll wake up to what life is all about."

"BILAL!" my dad yells. "I will not have you discussing such things in this house. Alcohol? I thought you had stopped drinking. You know it's *haram*, forbidden. And as for you, Shereen, stop speaking to me like I have a degree in English literature from Sydney University! How did I manage to breed such silly children, *ya Allah*! One thinks she's going to save the world by protesting about anything and everything, and the other has the intelligence of a squashed falafel. And my Jamilah? All she does is watch this OP or OC rubbish programme, or whatever it is called, and dye her hair yellow."

"Hey, don't pick on me!" I cry.

Shereen rolls her eyes at us and storms out of the room. My dad sighs and sits down, erupting into an angry monologue.

"A man comes home to his family and expects peace. I've been driving my taxi for the past thirteen hours and I come home hoping to spend some quality time with my family. And this is what I get? *Ya Allah*, give me guidance and patience. Jamilah, make me a cup of coffee, will you please? Make it strong. My back is sore from sitting all these hours."

"I don't know why you don't give the taxi up, Dad," I say. "You complain about a stiff back every night but you're still out there doing long shifts. I wish you'd get an office job."

"It's too late for that now, Jamilah," he says in a weary voice.

When my parents migrated to Australia in 1974, my father couldn't find a job, despite having a PhD in agriculture from the University of Beirut. His degree was highly specialized and the only work available would have required him to move us to the country. My parents weren't too keen on being the only Arabs in a remote country town.

So my dad swallowed his pride and worked in various factories. In fact, he initially worked as a taste tester at a beer factory. That didn't go down too well with my mother who, as a devout Muslim, never touched a drop of alcohol in her life. But my dad, who was a lax Muslim in those days, thought nothing of stockpiling the fridge with rejected VB cans left over from his shifts.

I make him a cup of coffee and go to my room. He's obviously not in the best of moods. In fact, I'd have difficulty convincing him to let me go to the corner shop. Tonight isn't the right time to attempt to work a miracle.

3

Years of hard work and dedication have enabled me to foster a talent for multitasking. I can pretend to be engrossed in my class work whilst simultaneously passing notes to Amy or reading a novel I've tucked away behind a textbook. Today I'm nurturing my talent further. I'm conducting internet research in my social studies class whilst chatting to various people on the ICQ chatroom. All of a sudden an envelope flashes at the bottom of my computer screen indicating I have a new addition to my email inbox.

The email is from **Rage_Against_The_Machine@hotmail. com**. I don't know anybody with that email address.

Amy leans over and looks at my screen.

"Cool email address," she says.

"I hope it's not a virus or some weirdo."

"Open it and see."

I open it and she moves back and focuses on her screen. She has her own multitasking to attend to.

From: Rage_Against_The_Machine@hotmail.com
To: Ten_Things_I_Hate_About_Me@hotmail.com
I'm in a school somewhere in Sydney at the moment.

I just noticed your email address in the Sydney ICQ chatroom.

I was compelled to email you. You see an email address like yours and the cosmic forces in the universe push their power into your fingertips and you suddenly find yourself emailing a complete stranger.

So what are the Ten Things?

This class is aggravating my didaskaleinophobia (fear of going to school). The one good thing about computers is that you can spend useful hours on Google looking up things that actually matter. Last week I learned that a teacher here who blushes every time a student speaks to her has ephebiphobia. That is a phobia meaning "fear of teenagers". She's clearly in the wrong profession.

Email me back quick, I'm bored.

My name's John, by the way.

I'm intrigued. I make sure that Mr Turner isn't hovering beside my desk and proceed to email John back.

From: Ten_Things_I_Hate_About_Me@hotmail.com
To: Rage_Against_The_Machine@hotmail.com

My name's Jamilah. I suffer from genuphobia (a fear of knees).

I'm also in class in a school somewhere in Sydney.

I am on the verge of suffering from narcolepsy.

What is narcolepsy you may ask. Well let me inform you, courtesy of my RESEARCH SKILLS, courtesy of my teacher, courtesy of his non-existent and naive brain.

Narcolepsy is a chronic neurological disorder caused by the brain's inability to regulate sleep-wake cycles normally. At various times throughout the day, people with narcolepsy experience fleeting urges to sleep. If the urge becomes over-whelming, individuals will fall asleep for periods lasting from a few seconds to several minutes. In rare cases, some people may remain asleep for an hour or longer.

My friend Liz is sitting next to me and has already contracted narcolepsy. Her head is bobbing up and down and her mouth is open. There is no dribble yet. I will let you know if any escapes. Is there a phobia of dribble? I'm sure you will advise me if there is.

The urge to sleep is becoming overwhelming because all I can think about is curling up on my sofa with a stack of movies and a block of chocolate. This class is killing me. The urge is getting stronger. And . . . str . . . on . . . g . . . e . . . r . . .

Zzzzzzzzzzzzzzzzzzzzzzzzzzz.

PS I don't know you well enough yet to tell you what the Ten Things are.

From: Rage_Against_The_Machine@hotmail.com
To: Ten_Things_I_Hate_About_Me@hotmail.com
Got to go. Add me to your address book and email me some
time.

4

Tonight I have madrasa, Arabic school. In addition to driving a taxi, my dad is on the committee that runs the after-school classes which are held once a week in a rented classroom in a public school in Wentworthville, which is about a twenty-minute drive from my house. My dad's on a personal mission to ensure I get no special treatment. So I have to attend class every Tuesday night. I've been attending since I was a kid; I conjugate verbs, do comprehension, write essays.

The best part about madrasa is that I'm part of a band. Each of us plays an Arabic musical instrument and we practise every fortnight. I play the *darabuka*, which is a drum. It's shaped like a goblet, and the trunk is made of wood or pottery, with the head made of skin. The trunk is usually decorated elaborately with inlaid designs in tortoiseshell and mother-of-pearl. My *darabuka* is black with mother-of-pearl designs. It's very funky. When you play the *darabuka* you strike the centre and edges of the head with both your hands, letting out a tremendous mix of heart-thumping beats.

After a long day at school, madrasa can get pretty tedious but I generally have a good time. Being in the band is awesome. Also, all the other kids in my class are wholly unconnected to my school, so madrasa is like a sanctuary for me. There I'm Jamilah. I play the *darabuka*, eat my Lebanese food and listen to Arabic pop music. I'm not a walking headline or stereotype. I'm just me.

We're running late to class this evening. My dad finished his shift a little later than usual and took ages getting ready. He usually dresses the same: stone-washed jeans hitched high up over his waist, shirts with colourful prints, and open-toe slip-ons. I'm not talking about trendy Ralph Lauren leather slippers. I'm talking big, floppy tan-coloured slippers with the masseur soles. Then there's the aftershave. He wears musk, and drowns himself in it. He smells like a lolly shop. Bilal and I have tried to buy him nice aftershave from David Jones but he doesn't really like it; he claims that musk makes him feel like a teenager. I fail to see the connection between adulthood and musk. I pointed that out to Dad and he nearly grounded me for backchatting.

"Couldn't you go a little easy on the musk, Dad?" I joke, the scent of it flooding my nostrils in the confined space of our car.

My dad is weaving in and out of traffic. "It is the most beautiful scent in the world!" he says in Arabic. He suddenly switches to English as a car cuts us off. "You son of za sister of za brother of a donkey!" he yells. "Get out of za way!"

I cringe and sink down in my seat. "Dad, relax will you?"

"Yes, yes, I will relax," he says dismissively.

"Can I ask you something, Dad?"

"Yes."

The heat in my body bubbles like soup on a stove. "There's a party this Saturday. . ."

He glances at me, one eyebrow raised. "Party? What kind of party? A study party? A poetry-reading party?"

"A normal party."

"Define normal."

"*Dad!* It's a normal get-together of teenagers where we listen to music, occasionally dance, huddle in groups and check out each other's outfits."

"You forgot alcohol, drugs and sex."

"It's not like that. That stuff will have nothing to do with me. Practically everybody in my class is going. I'll be home early!"

"I would feel more comfortable letting you sleep in a lion's den." He pauses and thinks for a moment. "Oh, and the lion hasn't been fed for a week."

"Dad," I groan. "I'm sick of being left out all the time. I don't have a social life."

"You're sixteen years old. Do you expect me to allow you to go? Do you think I left my brains in the trunk of this taxi? I know exactly what goes on in these places."

"Don't you trust me?"

"Trust, trust, you kids nowadays are fixated on this word. Trust will never be an issue between you and me. I take it for granted that I can trust my daughter."

"Then what's the problem? You know I don't drink and I'll never touch drugs!"

"A place where there is alcohol, drugs, relations between boys and girls is not an environment for my daughter."

"I'm not going to do anything wrong though."

"It doesn't matter how much perfume you have on, if you stand immersed in a rotten smell it will rub off on you."

"Oh, come on, Dad! You can't be serious!"

"I am. Not to mention that drugs can be put in drinks so that girls are easily violated. And you want me to send my youngest daughter out as prey? What has got into you, Jamilah?"

"I'm just so sick of being different. . . Why does Bilal get to do what he wants?"

"He doesn't. You know I disapprove of his lifestyle. But what can I do? I can't control him like I used to. He's a young man now. I can only scream so much."

"But if Shereen got up to what he did, it would be different. And she's older. So age has nothing to do with it."

"Girls have more to lose than boys."

"That's a double standard!"

"Nobody said society was fair."

"But I deserve fairness! My friends are allowed to go out and nobody has a sunset curfew like I do! I'm a freak!"

My dad sighs heavily. "It is absolutely out of the question."

We've arrived at madrasa and my dad parks the car. I jump out, slamming the door behind me.

"You're so unreasonable!" I cry, and storm off to class.

My Arabic studies and music teacher at madrasa is Miss Sajda. She's in her early forties but I think she's in denial. She wears thick black eyeliner like Cleopatra, lots of gold bangles, and leopard-print tops. Her hair is dyed light brown with strawberry blonde foils, and she teases her fringe so high that sometimes I want to yell out a warning for her to duck when she walks through the classroom door. She's pretty funky and down-to-earth. She's fiercely proud of her Lebanese heritage. At the same time, she's fiercely Australian.

Miss Sajda is a very close friend of my Aunt Sowsan (my dad's twin sister), so I occasionally mix with her outside of madrasa. Aunt Sowsan relishes any opportunity to fatten our family up with her superb cooking. Miss Sajda is usually included in the invitation because she's a divorcee and therefore, in Aunt Sowsan's opinion, is deserving of extreme sympathy and kindness.

The members of our band are Mustafa Moqbil, Samira

Abdel-Rahman and Hasan Celik. While we're waiting for Miss Sajda to arrive Mustafa announces to the class that he has a new rap number to perform.

Even though Mustafa, Samira and Hasan all play traditional Arabic instruments in our band, they're also wannabe rappers. They insist on starting most of their sentences with "yo" and ending their statements with "man". They also think they live in the "hood" and attend madrasa wearing Adidas from top to bottom, jeans ten sizes too big for them and bandannas. Mustafa also occasionally comes to madrasa with a band-aid on his cheek in reverence to the American rapper Nelly. Miss Sajda has never asked him to remove it. As far as she's concerned he has every right to look as ridiculous as he likes provided he can conjugate his verbs.

Mustafa, Samira and Hasan have a rap group called "Yo, Oz Iz In Da Hood". They invited me to join them but I declined.

The rap band consists of Mustafa (vocals), Samira (makes spitting noises into the microphone or blackboard duster, depending on the props available) and Hasan, who stands next to Samira, doing the whole rap thing with his fingers and offering the occasional "yo" to beef up the chorus.

"We came up with this last week," Samira says. She grabs a pencil case and starts making spitting noises into it in an attempt to create some rhythm and beat. Hasan begins walking up and down in the foreground. He has that "I'm too cool not to bounce when I walk" thing going on; his head is low, his knees are bent, his back is curved and his fingers are

35

in strict rapper mode, slicing and jabbing the air for no apparent reason. Mustafa coughs, looks at us with a serious, contemplative expression on his face, and then launches into the lyrics

"Yo, whassup?
Guildford niggers in da house
MCM is my name
"Yo" (interjection by Hasan)
Cops always out to lay the blame
They try to take away our pride
Cos they confused by their lies
They see us with our spikes
And they try to trample on our rights
"Yo" (another interjection by Hasan)
Maybe if we were white
They wouldn't put up such a fight
Yo whassup with that?
"You tell em gangsta" (Hasan again)
I tell ya, whassup with that?"

The class erupts into cheers and we all burst out laughing. The three of them take a bow, clearly enjoying the attention. Miss Sajda walks in and looks at us with amusement.

"I see that you're all being well entertained," she says, smiling at us. "Too bad you have a pop quiz on the history of Muslim immigration."

We all groan.

"Muslims have been in Australia from as early as. . .?" She stands over my desk and I look up at her.

"Um . . . since the time you could buy a kebab from a van at a petrol station?" The class laughs and Miss Sajda raises her eyebrows.

"Not exactly the answer I was looking for. Anyone want to bless me with an intelligent response?"

"The sixteenth century," Liyaana Donya answers. "Makassan fishermen from the east Indonesian archipelago visited the north coast of Western Australia. . ."

"How fascinating," Samira whispers to me in a bored tone.

"Jamilah, can you tell us how many English words derive their root from Arabic? Jamilah? Woo hoo! Earth to Jamilah!"

Her voice startles me out of a daydream in which I'm at George's party enjoying Peter's attentions. "Um . . . I'm not sure. . ."

"Over nine hundred," she says. "Can you give us an example?"

"Not really, sorry."

"Hmm . . . I am deciphering that somebody has had a bad day. But that's OK. Everybody's entitled to resent my class at least once a month." She winks at me and I smile back gratefully. "Now let's look at the word *decipher*," she continues. "The word cipher means zero in Arabic, which was used as a prominent symbol in early secret codes. . ."

She doesn't address me for the rest of the class. Later she approaches me, pulling up a seat beside me.

"You're not yourself today," she says.

I shrug my shoulders. "Just some personal stuff."

"Anything I can help with?"

"Nobody can help. My dad is a really stubborn person."

"What happened?"

I want to confide in her but I clam up. I don't expect her to understand. I don't want her pity and I don't want to be lectured. So I tell her that I'd rather not talk about it.

"Well, feel free to talk to me at any time. I'm willing to listen to anything you have to say."

I thank her, even though I have no intention of taking her up on her offer.

5

The following night I start writing.

From: Ten_Things_I_Hate_About_Me@hotmail.com
To: Rage_Against_The_Machine@hotmail.com
OK, John, before I bother adding you to my address book, let's swap our VS (vital stats — in case you're one of those people who doesn't understand net talk).

And don't go telling me that you have a sixpack and hazel-green eyes, are going to become a professional footballer and are a leading champion of feminist causes. I am just so fed up with false identities (I've clearly got some CRB — chatroom baggage — which I can email you about some other time).

OK, in a nutshell, here's my intro. If you don't like it, we can simply delete each other's emails and move on, no hard feelings.

Right. Here goes.

My birthday is 3 September and I like handbags and dangly earrings.

My mum died of a heart attack when I was nine and, no, I don't want to do a deep and meaningful about it.

I live with the following:

- Surround-sound electric blue stereo system
- The DVD collection of *The Godfather* series
- A 2500 horsepower hairdryer and diffuser
- My dad
- A brother and sister:

  a) <u>Shereen</u>: Twenty-two years old. Majoring in politics at Sydney University.

  Used to have dreadlocks, now wears the hijab. She buys her T-shirts off the net to avoid manufacturers who use outworkers – in other words, total weirdo.

  b) <u>Bilal</u>: He just turned eighteen. He bleaches his hair and wears baggy pants. Firmly believes he's a chick magnet. Nearly gave my father a heart attack when he arrived home last week with freshly bleached spiky hair and a tattoo on his shoulder with all our names written inside the body of an anaconda.

PS (as in Physical Stats): I have big brown eyes and long eyelashes that need Maybelline X-Factor mascara to curl. I've got a bit of acne but it's not enough to warrant total high-school annihilation. I have curly hair which I often straighten into submission.

That's all for now.

PS (as in Postscript): Since we're totally anonymous I might as well tell you that I'm Lebanese-Muslim. I attend madrasa (Arabic school) once a week and I'm part of an Arabic band.

From: Rage_Against_The_Machine@hotmail.com
To: Ten_Things_I_Hate_About_Me@hotmail.com
The first thing I would like to do is to congratulate you on your acquisition of *The Godfather* series. It says a lot about a person's character (particularly a girl's) if they are a fan of the greatest trilogy on earth.

So, well done.

The second thing is that I like garlic on my kebabs; Petra in Jordan is on my Places To Travel list; and I know how to say *son of a bitch* and *move your car* in Arabic due to overhearing the constant arguing between my neighbours (two brothers).

The third thing I would like to point out is that we will never discuss hair or mascara again.

And please, I am begging you in the interests of human rights and world peace, would you kindly refrain from using chatroom vocabulary with me? Abbreviations, secret codes — I am sixteen years old and one month, not eleven.

So can you tell me the Ten Things now?

From: Ten_Things_I_Hate_About_Me@hotmail.com
To: Rage_Against_The_Machine@hotmail.com
Ahem. Where are your VS??? (I abbreviate. Deal with it or use your cursor and send me off to deleted items.)

From: Rage_Against_The_Machine@hotmail.com
To: Ten_Things_I_Hate_About_Me@hotmail.com
Only child. Anglo background. Grew up on the North Shore. I love peanut M&Ms. I hate reality TV shows. I've been to Thailand and Darwin. I hate most sports (except table tennis) but have an unblemished record of masculinity and heterosexuality. I'm addicted to cheese-flavoured rice crackers. I think seaweed-flavoured rice crackers are just wrong.
    Is that enough?

I'll have to continue the email session another time as Amy has just sent me five text messages in a row. She urgently needs help understanding an assignment we have due tomorrow on *To Kill a Mockingbird*. So I log off (it's good to play hard to get with guys, even if it's in cyber world) and spend the rest of the night on the phone with Amy discussing Boo Radley and Atticus Finch.

6

I notice Amy and Liz sitting outside a classroom. Liz has her arm slung over Amy's shoulder and Amy's head is down. I walk up to them and feel myself bump into an invisible wall. It knocks me straight in the face and I shrink back. There seems to be a hidden aura surrounding the two of them, repelling me, turning me away. They look at me and Amy smiles self-consciously. Her eyes are glistened wet and she quickly avoids my gaze. Then Liz laughs out loud. It's an awkward, unmistakably false sound. She's trying to slice a tiny space in the wall with her laugh, allowing me to peek in for just a moment.

"We were looking for you before," she says. We both know

she's lying. "We were just talking about the . . . assignment that's due for English."

"Oh, yeah, um . . . the one on *To Kill a Mockingbird*?"

"Yeah, that one."

I've clearly interrupted something. Something I'm not supposed to be a part of. I thought I was making progress with Amy. Who am I kidding? With Liz gaining a boyfriend, the only thing I've earned is a permanent lab partner, that's all.

I tell them that I've got to pick a book up from the library and we smile at each other. Clumsy, self-conscious smiles. Our friendship isn't designed for serious conversations. I'm not a part of arms over shoulders and advice sessions. I know my place and walk away.

Timothy drops a book titled *Mysteries of the Great Barrier Reef* as he tries to negotiate his way through the row of desks during home-room. It's his unlucky day. Peter happens to be beside him and he sweeps down and scoops the book up.

"Ooh! Let's see what the centrefold looks like!" he exclaims, holding up a double-page photograph of a coral reef. Some of the class burst out laughing, and Peter, finding an audience, presses on.

"Are these the kind of centrefolds that make you drool, Goldfish? This bit of coral is *sexy*, is it? Playboy too boring for you, hey?"

"The fish turn him on!" Chris cries.

"So what's your ideal fantasy then, hey Goldfish?" Peter

says. "If you're with a girl, do you get her to dress up as Nemo?"

There's an eruption of laughter and I sit in my seat, burning with shame at my lack of courage to say something.

And yet Timothy doesn't blush. He doesn't look agitated or offended.

He looks Peter directly in the eye and says, in a voice as cool as ice cubes: "Wow, Peter, you never cease to amaze me."

"Oh yeah?" Peter says, jutting his chin out arrogantly. "And why is that, Goldfish?"

"Because you keep talking to me, making all these comments, and you just don't seem to have worked out that I value your opinion about as much as I value contracting a fungal skin disease."

He grabs the book out of Peter's hands and sits down at a desk, ignoring the insulting voice calling out after him as though it was an irritating mosquito buzz. And then, without any hint of embarrassment or self-consciousness, he opens the book and studies its pages.

Amy calls me again tonight and I do my best to hide my surprise. We've never been phone friends. I immediately notice that her voice is as flat and deflated as a punctured tyre.

"What's wrong? You sound down."

"Nothing . . . just bored. . . What are you doing?"

"We've got people over. My dad's friends. They're in the

lounge room playing cards and acting like it's a Saturday night. I can't hear the TV properly."

"Your dad sounds so cool. I can't imagine my dad playing cards or having a good time with his friends."

There's a long pause and she sighs heavily.

Something's going on but I don't know how to break down the barrier.

It's uncharacteristic for Amy to be moody or depressed. In the time I've been friends with her she's always been one of those people who's generally upbeat. In stark contrast, I'm an emotional roller-coaster. If I receive a poor mark on an assignment or I've had an argument with my dad, I need a couch and a psychologist with a good threshold for pain. Amy, on the other hand, has a run-in with a teacher or misses the ball in PE and starts lecturing me about the "move on with your life" theory.

As it turns out, I don't get to find out. She abruptly ends the call and I'm left with the phone receiver in my hand, realizing, not for the first time, that I don't have a proper relationship with my so-called closest friend. We're like the two sides of a train track, comfortable in our parallel existence. We don't intersect or touch each other. But sometimes you need to collide. You need to crash and make an impact just to feel your friendship is alive. To feel that it's more than passing notes to each other in class and sharing hot chips at lunch time. I don't have any collision scars from this friendship. And as deliberate as that is, it's not something I'm proud of.

7

"I can't make it to the party," I tell Amy on the phone on Friday night.

"Why not?"

"We've got visitors." Gastro's too sticky a lie. A stab of guilt slices through me.

"Oh."

"Sorry to cancel on you like this. Why don't you ask Liz to meet Sam there? I'm sure she will if she knows you're on your own."

"Yeah, maybe I will."

I feel awful lying to Amy but I'm too embarrassed to tell her that my dad won't let me go. I don't want her to pigeonhole me as a poor, pitiful, repressed Lebanese girl. I know that my dad's strictness is cultural and religious, but I also know it has a lot to do with my mother's death as well, and the fact that he's bringing us up alone. I don't understand him. I don't always agree with him. But I know that I'm not a stereotype and I'll do everything in my power to protect myself from being seen as one, even if that means lying to my closest friend.

Another Saturday night stuck at home while Amy and the rest of my class live it up at a party. I wonder what Peter will say on Monday morning. Whether he'll think I'm a dag for not going.

I'm slumped on the couch trying to convince my dad not to go out and rent an Arabic DVD for an "educational movie night", when Bilal walks in the lounge room.

"Hey Jam, do you think I should wear the blue shirt or the striped shirt?"

"I think you should stop putting on ten litres of aftershave. I need a resuscitator now."

He grins at me. "Appeals to the chicks."

"Don't be rude, Bilal," my dad scolds.

"So which shirt?"

"Take me with you and I'll tell you."

"Some other night, OK?"

"You can go out with Bilal's friends when I wake up with a full head of hair," my dad says.

"If you disapprove of his friends, why do you still let him go out with them? Why is it so different for me?" I cry.

"One weekend," my dad says, looking up at the ceiling. "One weekend in which my daughter and I do not argue."

I groan. "Why do you treat us differently? I'm just as responsible as Bilal!"

"Because, my dear, he is older than you. And he is a boy. A very silly boy, I admit, but nonetheless a boy, and the rules of life are different for boys and girls."

"Hey! I'm not silly," Bilal cries.

"You dropped out of high school, and for what? To fix your friends' cars? There is no respectable future under the bonnet of a car!"

"Give me a break, Dad."

"So what you're telling me, Dad," I say, "is that Bilal can get away with anything just because he's a boy?"

"That's right!" Bilal says, laughing and ruffling my hair. "You belong in the kitchen."

I hit his hand away. "Shut up, Bilal, you're such a sexist pig! It's all right for you, you're not the one who has to sit in home-room on Monday and listen to all the stories. The only exciting thing I get to do on a weekend is channel-surf."

I jump out of my seat and storm off to my room.

"Hey!" Bilal calls out. "Which shirt?"

"Figure it out yourself," I shout and slam my door.

I wonder if I'll ever have a normal relationship with my dad. If we'll ever be able to understand each other; reason with one another. With family friends he's a different man. We went to my aunt's house for New Year's Eve. I wasn't allowed to go out with my friends because the city would be filled with drunks, syringes and testosterone. The adults set up the backyard with a big tent and tables full of food. There were three spits of lamb and about ten farms' worth of chicken. There was a stereo system blasting out Arabic music and everybody was dancing and going wild. Especially the dads after they'd had a bit too much to drink. Dad doesn't need a drink to get him dancing. When an old Lebanese folk song started playing we had to make room for him and the other men or we would have been crushed alive. And there was my dad, this normally brooding, serious man, kicking up his legs, dancing around the backyard, making jokes, entertaining guests.

I came home that night with the hope that the Dad I knew before my mum died had returned. But as soon as we entered the front door I received a lecture about talking to Rami, Uncle Hishan's son. Rami is reputedly "wild" and "indecent" because he owns a motorbike, smokes in front of the adults and has an eyebrow ring. The fact that I had a two-minute conversation with him about his law degree was beside the point.

I went to sleep wondering where that dancing, laughing man had gone.

8

From: Ten_Things_I_Hate_About_Me@hotmail.com
To: Rage_Against_The_Machine@hotmail.com

Thanks for the VS.

I'm so bored. I know you're probably out raving somewhere but I have to nag. I'm stuck at home decomposing from boredom. Saturday night TV sux. It sux even more when you know your friends are going to arrive at school on Monday morning with a whole bunch of exciting stories to tell about their weekend.

My dad won't let me go to a party tonight. I ditched my friend. I was supposed to go to her house and we were going to go together. I lied. I told her I had family stuff on.

The night is productive so far. I've managed to do the following:

1. Scratch Bilal's favourite CD (it serves him right for not taking me out with him)
2. Eat a packet of Scotch Finger biscuits with a cup of hot chocolate
3. Read and reread all my girly magazines. I've redone all the quizzes too (although I had to ignore my previous answers which were recorded in pen)
4. Give my dad lots of super-filthy death stares
5. Make a compilation of songs for my MP3 player

Oh. And a mosquito just bit me through my sock. Joy.

From: Ten_Things_I_Hate_About_Me@hotmail.com
To: Rage_Against_The_Machine@hotmail.com
Boredom! Boredom is when you enter your name into dictionaries on the web in different languages to see if you mean anything in another nationality. Boredom is when you read the instruction manual to your TV remote control. Boredom is when you sharpen all your eyeliner pencils and lip-liners and tie them up with elastic bands and rearrange your dressing table.

By the way, I also hate seaweed-flavoured rice crackers.

From: Rage_Against_The_Machine@hotmail.com
To: Ten_Things_I_Hate_About_Me@hotmail.com
So what's the deal with your dad? Why aren't you allowed to go to the party?

From: Ten_Things_I_Hate_About_Me@hotmail.com
To: Rage_Against_The_Machine@hotmail.com
Oh hi there! So you're home tonight too? I don't feel like such a geek now, haha.

My dad's the paranoid type. He has certain curfew rules and Saturday night parties don't fit into them.

From: Rage_Against_The_Machine@hotmail.com
To: Ten_Things_I_Hate_About_Me@hotmail.com
Saturday night parties don't fit into most parents' curfews. My mum has issues if I ride my bike at night. She thinks I'll be mugged. They're all paranoid. It's a parental prerequisite.

From: Ten_Things_I_Hate_About_Me@hotmail.com
To: Rage_Against_The_Machine@hotmail.com
Trust me. Nobody comes close to my dad. He has a Charter of Curfew Rights that hangs on our fridge door. He made me type it up and sign it. It's saved in Word as "COCR". When things are abbreviated you know they're serious.

From: Rage_Against_The_Machine@hotmail.com
To: Ten_Things_I_Hate_About_Me@hotmail.com
Sounds interesting. What does it say?

From: Ten_Things_I_Hate_About_Me@hotmail.com
To: Rage_Against_The_Machine@hotmail.com
Will you laugh?

From: Rage_Against_The_Machine@hotmail.com
To: Ten_Things_I_Hate_About_Me@hotmail.com
Of course I will. But I promise you it won't be a condescending laugh. It will be a "what a freak of a dad, poor girl, haha" kind of laugh.

From: Ten_Things_I_Hate_About_Me@hotmail.com
To: Rage_Against_The_Machine@hotmail.com
I'm basically subject to a sunset rule. I have to be home before it gets dark. And if I go out during the day, it's strictly females only. The only excuse I have to talk to a boy outside of the "education context" is if he's scanning my groceries at a supermarket checkout.

From: Rage_Against_The_Machine@hotmail.com
To: Ten_Things_I_Hate_About_Me@hotmail.com
That's rough. Is your dad in the military or something?

From: Ten_Things_I_Hate_About_Me@hotmail.com
To: Rage_Against_The_Machine@hotmail.com
No, although come to think of it, he did do compulsory military service when he was eighteen, back in Lebanon. That's where he was born.

There you go! You've solved the mystery for me! A year in an army barracks as a teenager sowed the seeds for my dad's obsession with rules on fridge doors.

When Dad migrated to Australia he worked different factory jobs, even though he has a PhD. He's been a taxi driver ever since I can remember. I wish he was more ambitious and got a job which allowed people to call him doctor. I wish he'd pursue a career that enabled him to work in an office with a Harbour view and bring home sophisticated stationery I could take to school and show off. Ha ha. It's just that I hate that he fits the stereotype of the ethnic guy driving a taxi when I know he's so highly educated. I want people to give him the respect he deserves.

Look at me gushing like this. You must think I'm a weirdo. Sorry. It's just that I don't get to open up much.

So what does your dad do?

From: Rage_Against_The_Machine@hotmail.com
To: Ten_Things_I_Hate_About_Me@hotmail.com
He's a lawyer. And if you want stereotypes, I'll give them to you. I'm the son of a rich, successful barrister who is resisting his father's efforts to get him following in his footsteps.

It's enough to put you into a coma.

A couple of nights ago my dad invited a judge over for dinner. In a pistachio shell, here's how it went:

Dad: Son, you know His Honour. Say hello to His Honour.

Me: Hello His Honour.

His Honour (looks bored): That's funny, son.

Dad (gritting teeth): My son, the comedian.

His Honour: Son, comedy will get you far in life. But a strong academic record, a law degree and persistence, that will take you to the moon.

Me: So what you're saying is that I should become an astronaut?

My obvious enthusiasm didn't go down too well with my dad.

From: Ten_Things_I_Hate_About_Me@hotmail.com
To: Rage_Against_The_Machine@hotmail.com
Judges visit you?? Your dad is a hot-shot lawyer? I want to collect a visa to your world. I can imagine what your mum looks like. She wears designer clothes and her hair is always up in an exotic French twist and she smells of Chanel 5 and drives a BMW. You probably live in an amazing mansion and you'll get a car when you turn eighteen and your dad will use his connections and get you a job in a top-tier firm.

I am officially jealous.

From: Rage_Against_The_Machine@hotmail.com
To: Ten_Things_I_Hate_About_Me@hotmail.com
Judicial dinners, lectures about legislative reform and sterile mansions are about as exciting as toe warts.

9

It's official. Liz and Sam are going out.

"He asked me on Saturday night," Liz tells Amy and I as we walk to class on Monday morning. "He said he's had the hots for me since last year but he only just got up the nerve to ask me out." She giggles. "You two should have come to the party. It was awesome."

"You didn't go?" I ask Amy.

"Nope."

"Why not?"

She shrugs her shoulders. "I wasn't in the mood. Some family stuff came up for me too." We enter our classroom and she takes a seat.

Peter walks up to me. "You didn't show on Saturday."

"I couldn't fit it in," I say in as casual a tone as possible. It works. He looks impressed.

"I had a lot on this weekend."

"Anything fun?"

"Oh yeah. I had a lot of fun. I'm just so tired now. It was full-on." He doesn't need to know that I spent all Saturday night on the computer emailing John and then watching DVDs. I'm wrapping myself in vagueness and to my surprise it's working to my advantage.

"Are you always this mysterious?"

I smile coyly. My insides are somersaulting but I'm trying to keep cool. I am so nervous and uncomfortable with Peter's attention. "So how was the party?"

"A couple of my ex-girlfriends were there. Mouthing it off as usual, developing nodules. They never shut up. You know what I like about you, Jamie?" He leans close enough for me to see the piece of lettuce lodged in his teeth.

"All the girls I've dated can't keep their traps shut. They're always out to prove themselves. You, on the other hand, aren't obsessed with the sound of your own voice."

News bulletin: I am not obsessed with the sound of my own voice because I don't have a voice. I'm stifling it beneath layers of deceit and shame.

Mr Turner arrives for history and assigns a research project about Gandhi. He's just returned from a holiday in India and is eating curry for lunch, humming Indian songs and threatening to retire to Bombay.

We're to work in pairs. I'm about to turn to Amy when

Mr Turner announces that he's already drawn a list of names.

"I want to avoid the usual friends pairing up. This class needs to mix more. So listen carefully while I read my list out: Chris and Samira; Tamara and Edward; Timothy and Jamie. . ."

I look up in surprise. I lock eyes with Timothy and he nods his head and smiles. I can't believe my bad luck. Being paired with Timothy is not exactly the way to earn popularity points. In my class, loserdom is generally contagious. As if to reinforce my feelings, Peter throws a piece of scrunched-up paper at me. It hits me in the ear and rebounds on to my desk. I pick it up and unravel it. *You poor thing. You're stuck with Goldfish.* He's drawn a picture of a fish in the corner.

I don't know what to write back. I don't want to be nasty just to earn his approval. But I'm too chicken to defend Timothy. I tear a piece of paper from the corner of my book and think about what to scribble back.

But I'm as blank as a freshly painted wall. I can't think of anything remotely witty or flirtatious to write. So I do the pathetic thing and ignore the note, turn my head towards the front of the classroom and avoid the potential for any eye contact with him.

After class I resolve to say something to Peter face to face. I have no idea what though. I'm relying on my brain to perform under pressure. I turn from my desk but my path is blocked by Timothy. Timothy is tall and handsome. His bag is slung over his shoulder, his head cocked to one side as he looks at me. "So I guess we should exchange numbers."

"Why?" I blurt out, distracted by Peter who is standing behind me, listening. My palms feel sweaty and I tug nervously at my hair. "Oh, yes, because of the project."

Timothy gives me a weird look and then smiles. "A short memory span, hey?" He raises one eyebrow and murmurs to himself: "Well, it looks like we're going to ace this assignment."

I chuckle uncomfortably, still conscious that Peter is eavesdropping. "Um, yeah." We exchange numbers and I start packing my books away. Peter walks past and flashes me a sympathetic look.

"You must be rapped, hey Goldfish? Mr Turner organizing the pairs saves you the hassle of begging somebody to be your partner."

Timothy looks at Peter as though he were a cross-dressing cockroach. "Mate, sometimes I want to pity you. But even that would require me to acknowledge that you exist. You have as much relevance to me as a piece of lint on an unwashed sock."

Peter looks momentarily surprised. Then his eyes narrow in anger. "You'll always be a freak, Goldfish." He grins at me, convinced that he's won the confrontation, and walks away.

"You got to him," I say in an impressed tone.

He shrugs. "So when do you want to start working on this project?"

"Whenever."

"Are lunch times OK with you? I mean, the last thing I want to do is waste my lunch time in the library, but it's either that or after school."

If I work back after school I'll miss the bus, which will mean either Dad or Shereen will have to pick me up. I've done my best to avoid that from happening. If anybody sees Shereen with her hijab on, my cover will be exposed.

"I'd prefer lunch times too."

"OK, how about tomorrow? The sooner we get this thing done, the sooner I can go back to spending my lunch times thinking about my tropical-fish tank."

For a split second I believe him. It's a testament to the persuasive power of classroom gossip. Then I smile. But at the same time I'm worrying about what people, especially Peter, will think if they see me happily conversing with Timothy. Standard human decency has nothing to do with the situation. This is about my social standing.

It would have been easier if Timothy had had the personality of a spatula. I could have worked with him, looked bored and avoided anybody reaching the conclusion that I was enjoying my fate. Now he's gone and stuffed it all up by making me smile.

10

"On my cue! One, two, three!"

Mustafa starts playing the *daff*, which is an instrument similar to the tambourine. The sound of Samira's guitar creeps in, then Hasan and I join in too. We're practising with Miss Sajda and I'm loving every minute of it.

My *darabuka* is balanced under my arm and I drum down on the leather top with the palms of my hands, creating a deep, strong rhythm which echoes and reverberates in my chest. I feel a strange sense of calm and exhilaration. The sounds trigger memories of colourful weddings and Lebanese parties and dance floors and live bands and belly-dancers. I get lost in the beat of the drum as my palms move faster and then slower; one beat, then two, then four quick beats, then back to one. My palms coax the sounds from the leather, and beads of sweat line my forehead as our music becomes more intense.

This is where I belong, I think to myself. This is who I am.

When we've finished we gather around Miss Sajda. We're all on a high. We're skateboarding in the sky, our voices rapidly rising over each other's as we voice our delight with our performance.

"Man, we need to get professional!" Mustafa says. "We're too awesome to be stuck in a primary school classroom!"

"You got that right, bro," Hasan says. "I want an audience. I want to feel a crowd."

Miss Sajda laughs. "At the risk of encouraging your immodesty, I have to say I agree with you. You all play beautifully."

"We're fully sick, Miss Sajda," Samira says.

Miss Sajda grins. "How somebody who weaves notes of poetry out of the *oud* can describe her performance as *sick* is beyond my generation."

"You've got to get with the vocab," I tell her.

"No thanks," she says. "I'll stick with the dictionary for my definitions."

"So what do you think, Jamilah?" Mustafa asks me. "Do you want to try and get some gigs? We haven't had much luck getting gigs with Oz Iz In Da Hood."

"I can't imagine why," I say. "You're not exactly *Pop Idol* material."

Samira and Hasan giggle. Mustafa looks at me, grins and then launches into a song.

"Yo! Pop Idol is not my pleasure
I seek higher things as my treasure
I don't need to be judged or adjudicated
Just to get a TV channel rated."

We all burst out laughing.

"Don't knock our talent, Jamilah. We'll get there one day. We've just got to persevere, that's all. But this band we have going here has real potential."

"My dad will never let me." I'm not embarrassed to talk about my family life to my friends at madrasa. They've never ridiculed me or made stereotypical assumptions about me.

"How about you leave your dad to me?" Miss Sajda says.

"Are you *serious*?"

"I'll do my best."

I make a silent prayer to God to lend Miss Sajda a helping hand.

"Your serve," I tell Amy. It's PE and the two of us are playing squash. We paired up after Liz and Sam ran straight to a court together, Liz flashing Amy an apologetic smile.

"What do you think about Liz and Sam?" Amy asks me as she bounces the ball with her racket.

"I still think Sam is intimidating."

"In what way?"

"In the same way Peter is: cool, popular, confident. You

feel like you have to come up with something brilliant and witty whenever you talk to them."

"Peter and Sam are good friends, you know." She looks at me slyly.

"Yeah, I know. What's with the look?"

"What look?"

"The one you just gave me."

She gives a short hoot of laughter. "Don't be so paranoid."

"Don't be such a tease."

Amy raises her racket to serve and then lowers it and laughs. "You're right. I did give you a look. Peter's paying a lot of attention to you lately, isn't he?"

"Yeah . . . and it's weird and totally unexpected."

"He has power in the classroom. The computer geeks hang off his every word, even when he's making fun of them. Ahmed and Danielle's gang say they hate him but I reckon they secretly crave his approval. He can even make his enemies care."

I think for a moment. "Not Timothy."

"Huh?"

"Timothy couldn't care less."

"Yeah, well, not all of us have the luxury of being so totally unaffected by other people's opinions."

Suddenly the door slams open and Liz falls into the court. Sam is close behind her, grabbing her and kissing her neck. Liz squeals at him to stop, but she's laughing and he continues.

"Get your own court, will you?" Amy cries. "Or maybe a room."

Liz looks at us and grins. "Sorry, guys. We just came to see if you wanted to skip the rest of PE. Sam, Peter, Chris and I are going down to the oval for a smoke. We'll be back before the bus comes to pick us up."

"Since when did you smoke?" I ask.

"It's not a habit," she says defensively. "But I don't mind one here and there."

"News to us," Amy says, pursing her lips as she stares at Liz.

For a moment Liz looks uncomfortable, but then Sam throws an arm around her shoulders and draws her close to him.

"She hated it at first but now she's a pro. So are you two coming or are we going to waste the rest of the hour between four walls?"

"Thanks for the offer," Amy says, "but I'll take the four walls."

I glance at Liz. She's avoiding eye contact with Amy, whose face is etched with disappointment.

"What about you, Jamie? Peter will be there." Liz gives me a knowing look and I feel myself blushing.

"Um . . . no thanks. We've got a good game happening here."

Liz has became part of the cool crowd and half of me wants to throw down my racket and join her. I want Peter to admire my courage for skipping class. I want him to flirt with me. I was so close to saying yes, but I didn't. Not because I knew it was wrong. Not because I was trying to take a stance. But because I didn't want to leave Amy alone. If the circumstances had been different, I think I might have said yes. And that's not because I like Peter. No amount of good looks can override the fact that he's as good-natured as a crocodile with a toothache. Nah, it's pretty simple. I might have said yes because sometimes wanting to be cool can come at any cost.

Liz, Sam, Chris and Peter make it back to the squash courts without Mr Delerio noticing. We board the bus and I take a seat beside Amy. Liz passes us on her way to the back row and pauses.

"We got away with it!" she whispers to us and winks.

"Congratulations," Amy says in a tight voice.

Liz looks as though she's going to say something, but then offers us a flippant smile and walks away to join Sam.

I'm staring out the window when I hear Nicholas Kastani cry out, "Give it back!"

I turn around and see Peter holding Nicholas's Discman. He has the headphones over his ears and is laughing hysterically.

"What is this? Greek music?"

"Congratulations, genius," Nicholas says. "Got a problem with it?"

"It sounds like the guy's coughing his words." Peter starts gargling out pretend song words. "You Greeks should stick to running fruit shops."

"That's enough, Peter," Mr Delerio yells out.

Chris, Sam and several other kids laugh out loudly. Ahmed, Paul and Danielle yell out abuse at Peter.

"At least my ancestors weren't convicts," Nicholas says, snatching his Discman out of Peter's hands.

I glance over at Liz. She's cuddled up in Sam's arms, smiling as she watches Peter in action. I wonder if she realizes how much she's compromising by being with Sam. I wonder if I would do the same if I had the chance to be with Peter.

11

"What's it like living without a mum?" Amy asks me today.

I'm taken aback by her question. Until now, my mother has been an off-limits topic. I can't imagine why she's suddenly presumed I'm willing to talk about her.

"It's hard. . ." I say, focusing my eyes on the floor and not her face. Then I turn to her and give her a clenched smile. "I really don't want to talk about it, if you don't mind."

She's taken aback but then smiles at me awkwardly. "Fine . . . no problem."

She doesn't press the topic and we revert to more familiar ground: celebrities, school gossip and music. Once again I've ensured that the train tracks keep on running parallel.

I really don't like to talk about my mother. I think about her all the time but I've never been comfortable opening up to anybody — including my family — about how I've felt since she died. My dad always makes prayers for her. If her name is mentioned he always asks Allah to rest her soul and grant her paradise.

The day of her death replays in my mind over and over. She picked us up from school. Bilal and I were in the back yard playing soccer. Shereen was in her bedroom listening to music. Mum was hanging the laundry on the washing line. She came inside. She told us to be careful not to ruin Dad's vegetable patch. She sat on the lounge-room chair. She called out to us to telephone Dad. She felt pain in her chest. She was tired. She closed her eyes. Bilal and I thought she was just whining about the housework. She told us again: "Call *Baba*." So Shereen called.

She opened her eyes. She looked at us. She said: "It hurts." She was a pious woman. She said: "I declare that there is only one God and that Mohammed is His last Prophet." She closed her eyes. And she never opened them again.

She was born in Beirut and died in Australia. If she had never boarded that plane in 1974, would she have lived longer? What would God's plan for her have been? From the moment of her birth God had her heading for that lounge-room chair. Some guy in a factory manufactured it with professional care. He put it together, nail-gunned the upholstery over it, wrapped it in plastic and shipped it off for sale. Nobody knew it would land in our lounge room and hold my mother in her dying moments. It tore her from our lives. I slashed it with a knife when we returned from the funeral.

My father grieves through memory. He is constantly reminiscing about his life with my mother. We can be eating dinner and he'll remember eating the same dish with her and go off on a tangent about an outing or conversation they shared. A smell can send him into a long story about the scent of freshly roasted chestnuts on their first cinema outing in Beirut or the smell of henna in her hair. When my mother was young, she had long wavy hair down to her waist, kissed raven-red from her dedicated use of henna powder.

My favourite stories are of Mum and Dad's engagement days. My dad sounds like an entirely different person then: carefree and full of spirit. Not bogged down with rules and traditions.

They met at a mutual friend's house in Beirut. My mum had been playing tennis with her girlfriend, Maha. Maha was married to Hatim, my dad's close friend. I'm pretty sure Maha and Hatim set the whole thing up. Mum arrived at Maha and Hatim's house and Dad was there, in his light blue flared pants, puffy white shirt (tucked in), afro hair and thick black moustache (AGH!). Dad says it was love at first sight for both of them. I asked Shereen to verify this. As the eldest, she was closest to Mum and a teenager when Mum passed away. Shereen flatly refutes Dad's claim. According to Shereen, our mother was attracted to Dad and thought he was funny, but it took several outings before she was convinced he was "the one". Dad still stands his ground. "The moustache was very handsome," he says.

Apparently my mother was a very bad cook in her newlywed days. She eventually became a whiz in the kitchen. I'm not able to personally testify to this given that I was nine when she died and my taste in food ranged from peanut butter on toast to hot chips. I can say that she could make a bowl of Cocoa Pops into a five-star meal.

I remember Dad was cooking roast beef one day and as he was garnishing the meat he suddenly burst into a fit of laughter.

"What's so funny?"

"I just remembered something."

"About?"

"Your mother. When we were engaged I took her on a picnic. She insisted on bringing lunch. At one stage I'd mentioned to her that one of my favourite dishes was roast beef stuffed with spices and garlic. She was so sweet. She tried to make it. Except she stuffed the meat with about five whole heads of garlic. She hadn't minced the cloves, she'd just shoved them whole into the meat! I nearly choked! Of course, I pretended it was the best I'd ever eaten. But we both stunk until December."

I love hearing stories like that. My dad's eyes light up as he wanders back into his past. I wish I could sit him down and ask him to tell me more about Mum. But something always holds me back. I don't want to admit how much it hurts or how much I need his memories. That's why I keep it all bottled up inside. It fizzes and fizzes until I'm ready to explode sometimes. So when Amy opens the topic up today, I resist the temptation to let it all burst out.

12

When I come home from school today Dad has a bundle of pension scheme brochures he needs me to read to him.

Ever since I was little, Shereen, Bilal and I would be my parents' interpreters. If there were letters to read, bills to decipher or forms to sign, our parents would rely on us to translate.

Now that Bilal spends as little time at home as he can and Shereen's busy changing the world, Dad seems to rely on me more and more. Last week it was insurance renewal papers. The other day it was a parking fine. It's child labour exploitation whenever his friends visit. Uncle Kamil brings me his immigration documents. Uncle Yusuf needs me to explain whether his daughter's report card is *really* recording an A+ average. (It is. She's a genius that girl.)

Sometimes I feel frustrated and embarrassed that my dad's English is still so broken after all the years he has been here. He can get by, of course. He drives a cab so he can obviously communicate. But sometimes I feel that people would take him more seriously if he were fluent. They hear his heavy accent and he's suddenly less Aussie.

My father talks to us in Arabic all the time, watching Arabic satellite channels, reading Arabic newspapers. Sure, he watches mainstream TV too. He insists on watching every single news programme and bulletin, even if they're back to back. But his writing and reading skills are still poor.

"Can't you get Shereen to do it?" I moan. I'm feeling too lazy for a translation exercise.

"She's not home from university yet. Please read them to me. It says here ann-an-re-re-port. That is important."

"Annual report," I say in a huff. I sit down next to him and go through the pamphlet. Half an hour later Shereen arrives home, crashing down on the couch.

"I'm so tired!" she exclaims, rubbing her eyes. "But guess what I got you, Jamilah?"

"What?"

"A friend of mine just got back from Egypt. She brought along a whole stack of new CDs. Ihab Towfeek, Amr Diab, Nancy Agram. All their new albums."

My eyes light up in excitement. "Wow!"

"I borrowed them from her. Do you have a burner at

school? You can take them with you tomorrow. Just make sure you bring them back."

"Don't you have a burner at uni? I'd rather not take them to school."

"Why not?"

"Because I'd never hear the end of it."

"What do you mean?"

"It's woggy music."

"Jamilah!" my dad cries. "You are not to use that racist word in this house. Do you understand?"

I look at him in surprise. "All I meant was that in my school you only announce your background if you're prepared to deal with people calling you a wog."

"The word wog might not necessarily carry with it the negative connotations we traditionally associate with it," Shereen says in a tone that would put Lisa Simpson to shame.

"There is no excuse to use such a word. It is an insult, even as a joke."

"Seriously, Dad," Shereen argues. "In America the word nigger in rap and hip-hop culture has metamorphosed." Shereen is oblivious to my dad's fallen jaw. "Contrary to the traditional derogatory meaning of the word, rappers and hip-hoppers use the word as a term of endearment. Wog has undergone the same transformation. I'm not saying I justify its use – I abhor typecasting individuals and creating social cleavages based on ethnicity, religion or race – but I can understand how—"

"Shereen," my dad interrupts in an impatient tone, spit flying off the tongue as the Arabic words shoot out of his mouth, "I haven't understood one word you are saying. Do you try to make me feel embarrassed that I don't understand all this university language you keep using?"

I resist a grin as I watch Dad's radar move from me to Shereen.

"Of course not, Dad," Shereen says, looking wounded. "I would never try to embarrass you. I'm just trying to explain—"

"Then go invest in an English to Arabic dictionary, spend two weeks in your room translating that speech you just subjected me to, and come back and we'll talk about it. Although I have no idea what this *rip* and *hippy-hoppy* music has to do with my youngest daughter using the word wog so casually!"

"But Dad, you can't deny it. We are wogs," I say.

"No we are not! When I came to this country people would call you a wog and spit at you! It is offensive. You are an Australian, not a *wog*."

"Well, Dad, most people don't think that way. At my school if you speak two languages or have dark skin or don't celebrate Christmas, you're never really accepted as an equal. That's why keeping a low profile is the best option."

My dad almost falls off his chair. "You should be proud of who you are, Jamilah! You can be Australian and still have your heritage and religion. They are not at war with each other. Why is this life always like a battlefield for you? You are Australian and Lebanese and Muslim. They go together, Jamilah."

"Sure thing, Dad," I say half-heartedly.

"You were born here. You were raised here. I am the migrant. And yet I feel more comfortable with my identity than you do!" He shakes his head in disbelief. "My struggles should not be endured by my children. That means we have not progressed. We have gone nowhere and learnt nothing. There's something very wrong with that."

It's one of the rare occasions in my life that I can see that my dad has a point.

13

We're at Aunt Sowsan's house for dinner tonight. Aunt Sowsan is older than my dad by six minutes. She acts as though this gives her a licence to boss him around. She tortures him with lectures about watching what he eats, keeping up with his exercises for the arthritis in his knee, quitting smoking and cutting back on his intake of *makhalil* (spicy pickled cucumber, radish, onion and carrot) because of his blood pressure.

Aunt Sowsan is married to *Amo* (Uncle) Ameen. They don't have any children. Maybe that's why she pours such lavish affection on Shereen, Bilal and me. She's always coming over and cooking us surprise meals.

She remembers each of our birthdays, spoils us with presents at *Eid* and stopped us from fading away after Mum died.

As for Amo Ameen, he doesn't say much about anything at all. In the face of Aunt Sowsan's loud, bossy and controlling personality, he doesn't stand a chance. Amo Ameen is placid and inconspicuous and is content to smoke his *argeela*, his water-pipe, read his newspaper and eat through a bag of pumpkin seeds after dinner.

I'm sprawled on the couch, the top button of my jeans undone, as I try to draw in oxygen after savouring the delights of stuffed cabbage leaves, roast chicken and creamy potato bake (Aunt Sowsan apologetically claims that she was too tired to cook up a *real* feast tonight).

Amo Ameen and Dad are sipping mint tea, chewing on pumpkin seeds, and discussing New South Wales politics. Boring.

Shereen is sitting at the dinner table poring over a pile of photo albums.

Bilal has decided to grace us with his presence for a change. He doesn't really like family get-togethers, but the prospect of so much delicious food is sometimes too strong a temptation to resist. Plus, he has a soft spot for Aunt Sowsan. She can be pretty cool and easy to talk to – the complete opposite of my dad.

"So how many hearts have you broken since I last saw you?" she teases Bilal as she hands him a cup of tea and takes a seat next to me on the sofa.

He grins at her cheekily. "Oh, only about ten and there's one in the lifeline."

"Pipeline, you intellectual vacuum," I scoff.

"Boofhead," he says, and I throw a cushion at him and poke my tongue out.

Aunt Sowsan laughs and draws me to her chest, engulfing me in a hug.

"I can't see why you should be asking him about his girl-friends as though it's the most acceptable thing in the world," I say, pouting. "If I so much as received an innocent, friendly telephone call from a guy, Dad would ground me for life!"

"It's called a double standard, Jamilah," Shereen says without looking up from the photo album.

My dad, who hears me use the words "telephone call" and "guy" in the same sentence, has suddenly lost the urge to talk about Labour backbenchers. "Huh? What's this I hear? Who's calling who?"

"Nothing, Hakim," Aunt Sowsan scolds. "Nobody invited you into this conversation."

"Did you hear that, Ameen?" my dad says. "My sister is telling me to be quiet in front of my own children."

"You're right, Shereen," Aunt Sowsan says. "We're taught to apply the same rules to men and women, but unfortunately that's not how the world works."

"You're telling me," I mutter.

"We live in a patriarchal community," Shereen says, "which finds it convenient to manipulate the sacred text to satisfy the male ego."

For once, I'm on Shereen's side. Bilal, of course, isn't batting for our team.

"Another simple thought flash from our lovely sister," he says, rolling his eyes at her. He looks to me for support but it doesn't take him a second to work out I'm not impressed either.

"I'm only joking, Bilal," Aunt Sowsan says. "If I knew you were playing up I would personally show each and every one of your girlfriends the photo I have of you as a toddler running around the house with nothing but a plastic bowl on your head!"

He grins. "So what? I was as sexy then as I am now."

I groan.

"Shereen has a point though," Aunt Sowsan says. "If you look around the world there are so many societies in which Muslim women are oppressed. The Koran has been manipulated and abused to exploit women."

"Do not blame the Koran, Sowsan," my father says.

"I'm not blaming the Koran, Hakim," Aunt Sowsan says. "I'm blaming men. If they were faithful to the Koran we wouldn't see such oppression. But there are men who find it useful to misread, misquote and take things out of context to deny women their God-given rights."

"Do you want to know what the problem is?" I ask.

My dad smiles. "Tell us, Professor Jamilah."

"Our community always focuses on *female* behaviour. Guys get away with defying the rules but they're always forgiven. You pretend not to know that Bilal has girlfriends and that he drinks and parties."

"Hey, don't pick on me!" Bilal says.

"Well, it's true. You're openly proud of it. It's hypocritical."

"Don't be rude, Jamilah," my dad says.

"But Dad! You can't even accept me having friends who are guys, and yet Bilal has girls calling him all the time. And you can bet your life they're not talking about human rights or social welfare policies."

"In every society, Eastern or Western, a man's fall from grace is different to a woman's. That's just a fact of life. I'm trying to protect you because you're more precious."

"You're equating friendship with the opposite sex to *falling from grace*?"

"No. But our community can be harsh, Jamilah. People talk, and they talk rubbish. We have to live with that."

"Who cares what people say? If I'm not doing anything wrong, why should I care?"

My dad sits up higher in his chair, his face reddening as he gets more agitated. "Because, like it or not, gossip can ruin people. Look at Bilal here. Already people are talking about his hopeless future and how no girl will want to marry him."

"My future is not hopeless!" Bilal says, angry now. "I've told you a million times, I want to be a mechanic."

My dad waves his hand dismissively. "Son, that is not a career! That is a teenage pastime. People see that I have a PhD but my son plays with cars."

"He's good at what he does, Dad," Shereen says.

"You are in no position to defend him, Shereen," my father says. "Where is your future? You scored the highest in your Year Twelve examinations of all our friends' children. And yet you choose to do an arts degree. You could have done law or medicine. People ask me if you want to be a painter!"

"Dad! They're hopeless! An arts degree is a *humanities* degree."

"But where will it lead you? All you are interested in doing is organizing protests. There is no future in that." My dad tugs at his moustache, clearly tense. "People think you are a radical! An extremist! That is not a light sentence in today's climate, Shereen!"

"Calm down, Hakim," Aunt Sowsan says gently. "Do not worry yourself over what Joseph and Yunus and Amina say. They will always talk. They are bored and stupid."

My father isn't convinced. "None of you understand that our family is under the microscope. Ever since Najah died people have been watching to see if I will do a good job, what will become of my children. I have every right to care!"

Shereen, Bilal and I don't respond. We stare at the floor, taken aback by our father's outburst.

Aunt Sowsan clears her throat and then says: "Hakim, you know that Najah would be proud of the job you have done in raising her children."

My dad cuts her off. "Enough!" he says, raising his palm in

the air. "I think we have thumb-sucked this topic enough. Let us talk about something else." Then suddenly he loses steam and seems to deflate in his chair. He sighs heavily, picks up his cup of tea and asks Amo Ameen to raise the volume on the eight o'clock news.

14

From: Rage_Against_The_Machine@hotmail.com
To: Ten_Things_I_Hate_About_Me@hotmail.com
Have you ever been to Lebanon? What's it like?

From: Ten_Things_I_Hate_About_Me@hotmail.com
To: Rage_Against_The_Machine@hotmail.com
I was only seven so I don't remember much. I can remember that my grandma had a huge pile of Mars bars in her refrigerator and boxes of Kellogg's cornflakes, which she had bought at a ridiculously expensive price just so we'd feel at home.

So what are you like at school? Are you popular? An introvert or an extrovert? Are you a teacher's pet?

From: Rage_Against_The_Machine@hotmail.com
To: Ten_Things_I_Hate_About_Me@hotmail.com
Popularity is relative. I'm not trying to be pretentious, but that's the way I see it. You can be popular amongst a group of computer nerds but unpopular amongst the footy stars. Last year a chubby kid, Daniel, was getting picked on by this jerk in my class during a volleyball match. Daniel's pretty overweight and he can't reach the ball to save his life. It pissed me off, though, because he's a really decent bloke. Wicked sense of humour, smart as anything. The jerk — his name was Bobby — made Jessica Simpson look like Einstein. So I tripped Bobby over and he fell flat on his face. Sealed my unpopularity with Bobby, cemented my popularity with Daniel.

Moral of the story: If you're going to trip somebody over, make sure you can outrun them when they manage to get up again. I earned myself a pretty good punch in the gut for that!

From: Ten_Things_I_Hate_About_Me@hotmail.com
To: Rage_Against_The_Machine@hotmail.com
Ohhh, I've got myself a hero for an email buddy. So you're sweet as custard and can't run. Where have you been all my life, John?!

From: Rage_Against_The_Machine@hotmail.com
To: Ten_Things_I_Hate_About_Me@hotmail.com
So how about you? Do people lay the red carpet out for you at school, or do you spend each night agonizing over who you'll sit next to in class tomorrow?

From: Ten_Things_I_Hate_About_Me@hotmail.com
To: Rage_Against_The_Machine@hotmail.com
Seeing as you're totally anonymous to me, it can't hurt to tell you that nobody at my school knows about my background. That's why I'm not known as Jamilah at school. I anglicize my name. And dye my hair.

From: Rage_Against_The_Machine@hotmail.com
To: Ten_Things_I_Hate_About_Me@hotmail.com
I don't understand the anglicizing the name/dyeing hair thing. Explain.

From: Ten_Things_I_Hate_About_Me@hotmail.com
To: Rage_Against_The_Machine@hotmail.com
What if I told you I want to be a pilot when I grow up?

From: Rage_Against_The_Machine@hotmail.com
To: Ten_Things_I_Hate_About_Me@hotmail.com
I'd call the Intelligence services.

From: Ten_Things_I_Hate_About_Me@hotmail.com
To: Rage_Against_The_Machine@hotmail.com
You're just playing along with me. What would you really think?

From: Rage_Against_The_Machine@hotmail.com
To: Ten_Things_I_Hate_About_Me@hotmail.com
Female pilots are sexy.

From: Ten_Things_I_Hate_About_Me@hotmail.com
To: Rage_Against_The_Machine@hotmail.com
Oh shut up.

From: Rage_Against_The_Machine@hotmail.com
To: Ten_Things_I_Hate_About_Me@hotmail.com
So you live two lives?

From: Ten_Things_I_Hate_About_Me@hotmail.com
To: Rage_Against_The_Machine@hotmail.com
Pretty much. To everybody at school I have no cultural or religious baggage. I wish I could be me but I'm too scared.

I've learned to adapt, like a chameleon changing its colour to blend with its environment. That chameleon's got the right attitude. Stick out and you've got no chance of survival.

From: Rage_Against_The_Machine@hotmail.com
To: Ten_Things_I_Hate_About_Me@hotmail.com
Doesn't pretending to be half an identity irritate you?

From: Ten_Things_I_Hate_About_Me@hotmail.com
To: Rage_Against_The_Machine@hotmail.com
OK, I'm ready to share my list with you now.

Ten Things I Hate About Me

1. I was born and raised in Oz but people still assume I was born under a camel in a cave in a desert in the

Middle East to parents who belong to a tribe with Osama Bin Laden genealogy.

2. As a Lebanese Muslim, we're only always *randomly* held up at airports (it's *randomly* happened to my dad and I every single time we've flown to Perth to visit my uncle).

3. The only introduction most people have to my LM culture is through headlines about terrorists under pictures of men with monobrows, missing teeth, back hair and guns.

4. I want the right to apply for a pilot's licence or own fertilizer or have a non-mainstream opinion without being blacklisted. (This is all theoretical. I actually want to be a dentist or primary school teacher when I grow up.)

5. I'm one person at school and another person at home (the kind of split personality that would make a Gemini look stable).

6. I'm low enough to be embarrassed to be seen with my sister at school because she wears the hijab.

7. A charter of curfew rights is stuck on our fridge door.

8. I'm treated differently to my brother.

9. I'm attracted to a jerk at school because I want to be popular.

10. I have brown hair, brown eyes, brown skin and curly hair. Totally boring.

So to answer your question: yes, pretending to be half an identity irritates me A LOT.

From: Rage_Against_The_Machine@hotmail.com
To: Ten_Things_I_Hate_About_Me@hotmail.com
This is what I have to say about your Ten Things.

You're setting yourself up for disaster. Sooner or later the curfew rules and taxi licence and hijab and bleached spikes and bilingualism are going to reveal themselves. They're going to crumple up at your feet and your friends will demand an explanation.

You're going to have to make a decision.

Will Jamilah finally get a chance to say something?

I feel like I have finally made a true friend.

Keeping your distance from your friends is exhausting. It means you're constantly acting, constantly choosing your words and thinking about ways to avoid exposing yourself. I can't afford to show them the real me. They wouldn't understand my culture or my religion. I've done everything I can to disassociate myself from being identified as a wog. Amy likes me as Jamie. She doesn't know about Jamilah who speaks Arabic and goes to madrasa and celebrates Ramadan and plays the *darabuka* and can cook Lebanese food and has a strict dad.

I wish I could talk in capital letters at school. Use exclamation marks and highlighter pens on all my sentences. Stand out bold, italicized and underlined. At the moment

I'm a rarely used font in microscopic size with no shading or emphasis.

But at least I've started on a new page with John. The honesty of our friendship is so raw and real that sometimes I can't wait to open my inbox and step into a world where being Jamilah comes naturally.

Miss Sajda pulls me aside after class. I'm prepared for a lecture about the poor quality of my translation into Arabic of an article in the *Sydney Morning Herald*. To my surprise, however, she gives me a warm smile.

"He agreed," she tells me.

"No way!"

She grins back. "There was a fifteen minute interrogation session but I passed with flying colours. Of course, whenever we get an offer to play you will have to get his permission. That goes for Mustafa, Samira and Hasan too. Parental consent is imperative."

I jump up and down in delight. "I can't believe it! You're a miracle worker! He's the strictest parent on the planet!"

Miss Sajda shakes her head. "My mother, God rest her soul, would have taken that title. She was a very religious Catholic. My collars always had to be high, my skirts down to my ankles, my sleeves long. I had to come home directly from school. She even wanted me to marry as soon as I turned eighteen."

"Wow, that's young!"

"We lived in a very affluent suburb in Lebanon and my

mother was quite snobby. She was determined that I should marry into a wealthy family. One day a man named George Chaouk came to our home and proposed. He imported cars so he was very well off. I refused him, though, and my mother was furious. I was determined to go to university. I didn't want to be a trophy wife."

"Did your mum forgive you?"

"It took a while. You see, George's family was very active in my mother's church; rejecting George was a tremendous insult to them, particularly given the fact that I was only eighteen. They thought I was arrogant and too strong-willed!"

"My dad has always insisted that we're not to mention marriage until we have university degrees. I'm grateful to him for that."

"Well that's why I'm telling you my story. My mother restricted my freedom even when I was a university student. She was overly concerned about what people would say if I was seen at cafés or with male friends. But Jamilah, I learnt not to argue over the small things. I could handle restrictions on my clothes and the time I was expected home. I saved my energy for what mattered most to me – which was to gain an education."

"Education isn't the issue for me," I explain. "I just want more freedom. I can't even talk to a boy without him going off the deep end. He's completely caught up in how his friends will talk."

"I know it's hard for you. You see your friends with

practically no limitations to what they can do and you feel deprived."

"Sometimes I feel suffocated. I'd love to invite my friends home or go out to see a movie at night."

"Your father would have no problem opening his house to your friends. I'm sure he would love it."

"Ha! There is no way I would."

"Why not?"

I give her an uneasy look. "It's . . . embarrassing."

"What is?"

How can I tell her that I'm embarrassed to reveal myself to my friends? That as much as I love my identity at home and at madrasa, my relationship with my school friends is a constant struggle of deception?

I jump up from my seat and avoid her gaze. "I better get going or I'll be late."

She gives me a knowing look but I rush out of the classroom before she has a chance to say something.

15

I desperately need a plan of action. If I don't get some freedom or independence soon, I'll be stuck at home watching TV and surfing the internet until graduation. That's three years' worth of annoying commercials, unimaginative sitcoms and pointless Google searches. I can't bear it.

Several strategies for getting out of the house cross my mind. I could sign up as a volunteer cleaner at our local mosque. I could donate blood every weekend. Surely Dad couldn't forbid that!

I'm racking my brain as I sit in Bilal's car on my way home from the bus stop. Bilal's picked me up as it's raining. He takes me into a McDonald's drive-through. The girl serving us doesn't look a day older than me. As she hands Bilal our order I have a sudden revelation. I almost knock the drink out of Bilal's hand as I lean over him and ask her how I can apply for a job. She gives me an application form and Bilal looks at me like I have momentarily had my brain juiced at a Boost bar.

"Are you running a fever?" he asks as we drive off.

I chew on my fries and bounce up and down excitedly in my seat. "That's it! It's my ticket to freedom! A casual job! I can finally have a life outside school and home. I can earn some money! I can have an extended curfew! I can discover the recipe for Big Mac sauce and find out if the salads are really low-fat!"

He shakes his head and turns the music up. "As if Dad will let you. He gave me a hard enough time about working at Red Rooster when I was in school."

"That's because you spent about ten minutes per annum at your desk studying. He knew you were looking for any excuse to get out of doing school work."

"Do you mind?" He looks at me in digust.

"Whssfdgt?"

"You have half a burger and ten fries in your mouth and are insisting on having a conversation with me."

I grin at him and his head jolts to the side. "Close your mouth! Ugh! You are so revolting."

"I love showing you my mature side," I say, laughing. "Anyway, you have to help me with Dad. Come on, we'll practise. Let's do a role-play. You act as Dad and I'll be me."

We're stopped at a traffic light and he bangs his head on the steering wheel and groans. "All right," he says in a defeated tone. "Start."

"Dad, I'd like to become more responsible and mature and learn the value of money."

Bilal pretends to choke but I ignore him. "Accordingly, I am seeking your permission to work on a casual basis at McDonald's family restaurant."

"NO!"

"Bilal, he wouldn't yell yet. The yelling comes later. At first he's calm and that's the deadly part. Sheez, has it been that long since you've done the begging routine?"

"Yeah, I don't ask any more. I just do."

I throw a French-fry at him and he nearly rams a traffic light trying to stop it from "soiling" his car interior.

"Please hear me out, Dad," I continue. "Everybody knows that having a casual job at a fast-food establishment looks good on your resumé because of the discipline and training you receive. Also, I'm highly dedicated to my studies, so if I have a job and good marks that also shows my maturity and conscientiousness."

"What's being unconscious got to do with it?"

"Never mind," I say, rolling my eyes at him. "Just play Dad."

"Can I yell now?"

I look at him and smile wearily. "Yeah, the yelling would start right about now."

*

Aunt Sowsan is at our place for dinner. After Shereen and I pack the dishes away and make tea for Aunt Sowsan and Dad, Shereen goes to her room to do an assignment. I sit down next to my dad and say a silent prayer that he won't freak out on me.

I don't even get a chance to indulge in my spiel about good marks and holding down a job. He hears me say "casual job at McDonald's" and shakes his head. I lose my cool. A sea of rage crashes through me and I leap out of the chair, flinging my arms around furiously. "Why do you always have to say no automatically? Not once have you ever given me the chance to put a case to you! You don't care one bit about what I think or feel, you just treat me like some kid!"

"No I don't, Jamilah."

His voice is cool and calm and I want to scream. The anger and frustration is suffocating me, moving up my throat like a bust water main, threatening to flood the room when it finally gushes out.

"Yes you do! No matter what I ask, you always say no. I never get the benefit of talking to you about it, or even the slightest indication that you value what I have to say. It's just a big fat automatic no."

"I know what's best for you."

I stare at him for a moment, my chest heaving up and down. Aunt Sowsan is quiet and hasn't intervened.

"How can you know what's best for me? You never talk to me. You never listen to me. You just give me orders."

I run out of the room and into my bedroom, slamming the door behind me. I wait for him to storm after me to lecture me about "being rude", but he doesn't.

I overhear him arguing with Aunt Sowsan. I can't make out the words clearly though. I hear Dad say "...don't tell me ... raise..." and Aunt Sowsan saying "...nothing to be worried about ... let her go ... couple of days..."

Aunt Sowsan knocks on my door an hour later and asks if she can come in. I ignore her and pretend to be asleep. I'm not in the mood for hearing how I have to "understand my dad" and "see things from his point of view".

I can understand why he won't let me go to under-age clubs or stay out late with my friends. I will give him that much. But what I can't understand is why somebody who experienced so much in their own teenage years wants to deny their daughter any experiences of her own. My dad always tells us about all the jobs he worked when he was a young boy growing up in Beirut.

Sometimes I find my dad in the quiet of the night sitting in his armchair, puffing away at his water-pipe and drinking his sweet mint tea. The television is switched off but there is a peculiar dreamy smile on his face as he stares at the blank screen. At those times Dad tells me what his life was like growing up in Beirut before the civil war. He becomes lost in his Arabian reverie and talks to me as an equal, as an audience to be entertained and amused, not a subject to be disciplined and tamed.

I listen to him and I feel jealous, wondering what stories I will have to tell when I'm his age.

Dad drops me off to the bus stop in the morning as I've slept in and I'm running late. The first half of the journey is silent except for the ABC news and the occasional sound of my dad's smoker's cough. As we get nearer to the bus stop, my dad turns his head towards me and says: "Which McDonald's?"

I dig my fingernails into my hands to stop myself from gasping.

"Parramatta."

"How many days a week?"

"Two. They're after-school shifts. And if I'm really good I can get Saturday night too and it's double pay."

We've arrived now and I hold my breath in anticipation of his response.

"I'll think about it," he says and I nod, not daring to push my good fortune. I lean over, whisper a thank you, then kiss him goodbye and jump out of the car.

16

I'm unpacking my books for English when Peter approaches my desk, smiles, and slides into the empty seat beside me. "Who's your favourite rugby team?"

I giggle nervously. "Oh, I'm not really into rugby."

"Then you should barrack for the Parramatta Eels. They're champions. Don't ever be a Canterbury Bulldogs fan. They are our mortal enemy."

I laugh and raise my eyebrows at him. "They're all the same to me."

He slams his hand across his forehead dramatically. "You're killing me here, Jamie! There is a fundamental difference. It's of religious significance that you appreciate this. The Eels are legends. The Bulldogs are losers. Don't ever forget that."

I find myself suddenly feeling confident and forgetting how cruel Peter can be. All I can think about is the fact that people are watching us.

"Oh, I don't know, Peter, they're both just a bunch of oversized buffoons who kick a ball and smash into each other. Oh yeah, and who wear shorts one size too small. I'm sure there are some anatomical risks there."

He bangs his head on the desk and moans. "You need to be re-educated."

"Mr Clarkson, is there something you'd like to share with the class?" Mr Arnold yells out from the front of the room. "Unless your conversation is about Charles Dickens, I suggest you zip it or you will be getting excited about lunch-time detention with me. Understood?"

The rest of the class boos and Peter stands up and takes a bow, grinning down at me.

"That's enough of your antics, Mr Clarkson," Mr Arnold says. "Now sit down and try to apply yourself, as hard as that may be for you."

Peter sits down, a confident grin plastered on his face as he soaks up the attention.

As we pack up our bags after class he leans over towards me. "The next time there's a match on between the Eels and the Bulldogs, you should come. You can't be a Sydney person unless you get into football. You may as well move to another state." He winks at me and walks away.

*

Liz applies her interpretive skills to my conversation with Peter and instantly concludes that he wants to ask me out on a date.

"He was definitely flirting," Liz says. "I saw you both. The whole eye-contact thing when he got into trouble. When a teacher humiliates you, the first person you look at says a lot about what you think about them. Peter sought your eyes out instantly."

I smile shyly. The more attention Peter gives me, the more the Jamilah in me fades away. I begin to believe my lies. That I'm a girl without cultural or religious baggage. That I'm Peter's type.

"Would you say yes if he asked you out?" Amy asks.

I shrug. "I don't know. Anyway, it's really unlikely to happen. Sure, he seems to be flirting with me, but we're not on the same level. He wouldn't risk his reputation."

I've never had a steady boyfriend. I've been asked out but I've always turned guys down. It's just too complicated. My dad would literally have a heart attack if he found out. It wouldn't be worth the risk. How would we go out? What if the guy called me at home? What if I got busted? Then there's the whole physical thing. Most guys consider it part of the relationship package. I've never kissed a guy. I've always chickened out at the last minute. The most I've done is held hands. I don't think that even counts as first base. The guy was George Fraser in Year Eight. I put a stop to that though. His palms had sweat pores the size of golf balls. I needed to walk around with a hairdryer after holding hands with him.

I cast my mind to an image of Peter and me walking hand in hand down the Year Ten corridor. I've made it. Everybody laughs at my jokes, and when the joke isn't funny I'm not a try-hard, I'm "cute". I'm guaranteed an invite to every party. My dad's rules don't apply in this fantasy. Girls huddle at recess and discuss how adorable Peter and I look as a couple. Guys treat me like one of the group. There's no booing when I miss the ball in PE. I'm Peter's girlfriend. I've cemented my position in the school hierarchy. I'm immune.

But even if the universal laws of probability were suspended for a day and Peter asked me out, he'd be asking *Jamie* out. He wouldn't look twice at Jamilah.

17

From: Ten_Things_I_Hate_About_Me@hotmail.com
To: Rage_Against_The_Machine@hotmail.com
Two all-beef patties, special sauce, lettuce, cheese, pickles,
onions on a sesame-seed bun.
   Guess what?

From: Rage_Against_The_Machine@hotmail.com
To: Ten_Things_I_Hate_About_Me@hotmail.com
You're hungry?

From: Ten_Things_I_Hate_About_Me@hotmail.com
To: Rage_Against_The_Machine@hotmail.com
I am officially a McDonald's employee.

Yippee!

From: Rage_Against_The_Machine@hotmail.com
To: Ten_Things_I_Hate_About_Me@hotmail.com
Do you realize how many kilojoules there are in your newly acquired profession?

From: Ten_Things_I_Hate_About_Me@hotmail.com
To: Rage_Against_The_Machine@hotmail.com
Don't ruin this glorious moment for me. By some miracle, my father has agreed to me working on a casual basis at Parramatta McDonald's and I want to hire a hot-air balloon and shout it out to the whole of Sydney!

This means freedom and financial independence and something TO DO on a Saturday night (assuming I impress the duty manager and secure a weekend shift).

From: Rage_Against_The_Machine@hotmail.com
To: Ten_Things_I_Hate_About_Me@hotmail.com
You'll get minimum wages and probably afford half a DVD a week and you call that financial independence?

You're easy to please!

From: Ten_Things_I_Hate_About_Me@hotmail.com
To: Rage_Against_The_Machine@hotmail.com
WARNING: Do not attempt to make another smart-arse comment about my new job, because I'm in a state of bliss at the moment and will track you down and thump you in the

head with a bottle of Evian if you do not congratulate me in the next email and tell me that I ROCK!

From: Rage_Against_The_Machine@hotmail.com
To: Ten_Things_I_Hate_About_Me@hotmail.com
Do I get any discounts on your shift?

From: Ten_Things_I_Hate_About_Me@hotmail.com
To: Rage_Against_The_Machine@hotmail.com
Yeah, leftovers.

I'm so excited. I can't believe my dad agreed. I'm determined to prove to him that I'm responsible and trustworthy. Maybe then he'll relax a little.

From: Rage_Against_The_Machine@hotmail.com
To: Ten_Things_I_Hate_About_Me@hotmail.com
Your dad doesn't seem so bad. I can accept that he goes off the deep end when it comes to the male gender and that he has some chronic fashion problems (masseur soles!). But he is obviously trying to cope bringing up a Puff Daddy try-hard son and the female equivalent of John Lennon. And then there's you. You'd be a handful.

I don't know. Your dad seems harmless to me. My dad's a son of a bitch. At least your dad goes a little deeper.

From: Ten_Things_I_Hate_About_Me@hotmail.com
To: Rage_Against_The_Machine@hotmail.com
Why's your dad a SOB? I get scared even writing that. I've

never sworn at my dad. It gives me chills to think what would happen if I did. My dad thinks "shut up" is a swear word (how old-fashioned is that?). "Say *be quiet*," he tells us. Like Bilal is really going to listen to a polite request for silent tonsil action when he's singing away to a Ja Rule song and I'm trying to watch a *Survivor* finale.

From: Rage_Against_The_Machine@hotmail.com
To: Ten_Things_I_Hate_About_Me@hotmail.com
He just is.

From: Ten_Things_I_Hate_About_Me@hotmail.com
To: Rage_Against_The_Machine@hotmail.com
Wow! Information overload. Restrain yourself! That essay was too much for my heart to take.

Listen to me, John. There is no way that I am going to do all the opening and sharing in this relationship. If you were my boyfriend I'd dump you for that pathetic "He just is". I'd make you pay for that ridiculous attempt to flush a topic down the toilet. I will not be the only one bitching about her family in this email relationship, got it? Now that it seems you may not have a perfect family, I want to see you pour out a good chunk of venom and spite and indulge in as much whingeing, whining and nagging you can come up with, and then some.

Did that penetrate your brain cells? Now let me see some keyboard action.

From: Rage_Against_The_Machine@hotmail.com
To: Ten_Things_I_Hate_About_Me@hotmail.com
All I can say is thank God you're not my girlfriend.

From: Ten_Things_I_Hate_About_Me@hotmail.com
To: Rage_Against_The_Machine@hotmail.com
Details required before normal conversation resumes.

From: Rage_Against_The_Machine@hotmail.com
To: Ten_Things_I_Hate_About_Me@hotmail.com
What's the big deal? I really don't want to have to do this.

From: Ten_Things_I_Hate_About_Me@hotmail.com
To: Rage_Against_The_Machine@hotmail.com
I'm waiting.

From: Rage_Against_The_Machine@hotmail.com
To: Ten_Things_I_Hate_About_Me@hotmail.com
Oh come on. Do you really want to hear a sob story? It's so
boring.

From: Ten_Things_I_Hate_About_Me@hotmail.com
To: Rage_Against_The_Machine@hotmail.com
Clock is ticking.

From: Rage_Against_The_Machine@hotmail.com
To: Ten_Things_I_Hate_About_Me@hotmail.com
OK, OK. You know what? You are really stubborn.

Hmm, you want to know why I hate my dad?

Because he's sarcastic. All the time. Because he puts my mum down. All the time. Because he tells me I'm going to amount to nothing. All the time. Because he only cares about making money and he only visited my grandfather, my mum's father, in hospital twice when he was dying of cancer – less than ten minutes each time. He was busy with meetings, he said. Liar. Because he's the type that doesn't smile with his eyes and if you need five bucks he expects you to pay him back. But most importantly, because he cheated on my mum with some young law clerk and actually had the gall to tell me to mind my own business.

If I were to give my dad a Father's Day card, you know what I'd say? Thanks for being my sperm donor.

That's basically the extent of his contribution to my life. Satisfied?

From: Ten_Things_I_Hate_About_Me@hotmail.com
To: Rage_Against_The_Machine@hotmail.com
Oh . . . um . . . that's pretty rough.

You must think I'm pretty dumb, hey? Here I am complaining about my dad's job and my curfew and your dad cheated on your mum. You put things into perspective for me.

From: Rage_Against_The_Machine@hotmail.com
To: Ten_Things_I_Hate_About_Me@hotmail.com
Don't you dare start to pity me. This is exactly the reason I

wanted to avoid the topic. I swear if you don't email me back with a good whinge about your family you are going to deleted items. And guess what? I'm then going to send you off to *permanently* deleted items. Never to return.

Things better go back to normal between us. I want doom and gloom emails and apocalyptic visions of our future. Hey, you have a screwed-up family too! You're just as messed up as me, I assure you. OK? Do not get any perspective. I suggest you immediately, AS IN RIGHT NOW, go to your room and listen to some soppy love song and feel sorry for yourself. Cry a little if you must.

Deal?

From: Ten_Things_I_Hate_About_Me@hotmail.com
To: Rage_Against_The_Machine@hotmail.com
Marry me.

From: Rage_Against_The_Machine@hotmail.com
To: Ten_Things_I_Hate_About_Me@hotmail.com
On two conditions:
1) There be no reality TV shows allowed to screen at any point of the day in our household.
2) We have a *Godfather* trilogy night every three months.

From: Ten_Things_I_Hate_About_Me@hotmail.com
To: Rage_Against_The_Machine@hotmail.com
Actually, I've changed my mind. You never make any spelling

mistakes. That means you're probably the type of guy who irons his undies, colour-coordinates his wardrobe and always puts the lid back on the toothpaste tube. We'd be divorced within the hour. Let's just stay friends,

Speaking of appearances, how do I know you're not some cross-eyed, toothless, balding freak? We're just faceless, anonymous entities at the moment. But I'm not really into the exchanging pics with a stranger thing.

From: Rage_Against_The_Machine@hotmail.com
To: Ten_Things_I_Hate_About_Me@hotmail.com
Based on what I know about you, you're about an eleven out of ten in my mind. What's my score with you?

From: Ten_Things_I_Hate_About_Me@hotmail.com
To: Rage_Against_The_Machine@hotmail.com
Nine out of ten. You need to work a little harder.

18

My dad's mobile phone keeps on ringing and I yell out for somebody to answer it as I'm on the internet, emailing John. Nobody does and so I rush to the kitchen, where it's vibrating on the benchtop, and answer it myself.

Miss Sajda is on the other end. We go through the chitchat niceties for a couple of moments and then she asks to speak to my dad.

"So he's still home?" she asks when I tell her that he's taking a shower.

"Yeah, why wouldn't he be?" I ask in a puzzled tone.

"There's a staff meeting on at madrasa."

"But it's Saturday."

"We're discussing curriculum issues."

"Will it take long?" I ask hopefully.

The prospect of having the entire house to myself is always thrilling. I can turn the music up as loud as I want or watch M 15+ rated movies to my heart's content without having to glue my finger to the fast-forward button in case my dad happens to walk in.

The meeting is scheduled to finish late. My face erupts into a wide grin. I'll be the first to admit that it doesn't take a lot to get me excited.

"Don't you sometimes wish something exciting would happen in your life?" I ask Amy on the telephone.

It's eight o'clock and my dad is still out with the rest of the madrasa staff who decided to go out to dinner.

I'm sprawled on the couch in the family room, surrounded by half-eaten packets of crisps, a couple of cans of Coke, a dozen magazines and a collection of DVDs. I've been on the telephone to Amy for the past two hours, discussing our favourite movies and what we want to do when we finish school. It's the longest telephone conversation we've ever had.

"I'm sick of talking to you now," she says light-heartedly. "You've harassed me all afternoon."

"Hey, it's been a symbiotic relationship," I joke. "Your parents are out too and you're stuck home alone and bored. You need me as much as I need you."

"Anyway, being home alone isn't such a weird thing for me

lately. I like having the house to myself. I hate it when my parents are home."

"Why?"

"Because we're just one big happy family." Her voice is bitter and I ask her if everything is OK.

"Yeah, of course it is," she says in a dismissive tone. I'm about to say something but she cuts me off. "Liz has changed."

"In what way?"

"She smokes now. She skips school with Sam. The other day Sam was making fun of Simon because Simon's father came to the office. You know how he's Sikh? Well his dad was wearing a turban and Sam was making fun of him. I couldn't believe it but Liz was laughing along with him."

"That's horrible."

"I can't stand people who change themselves just to fit in."

"Yeah, I know," I mutter uncomfortably.

"It's such an act of weakness. Is Liz so desperate for a boyfriend that she has to erase her personality?"

I gulp hard. I so desperately want to confide in her. I want a friendship based on honesty and openness. But it's obvious that there is no way Amy will ever understand my situation. Or forgive me.

I was desperate for some excitement but now I take it back.

I want a refund on my words.

I want an IOU.

I don't want excitement.

I don't want adrenalin rushes and panic attacks.

I spoke too soon!

My world crashes down on me like the surf at Bondi Beach.

In home-room on Monday Mr Anderson announces that the Year Ten committee has finalized the details for the Year Ten formal scheduled for the end of term two, in June.

I freeze in my seat.

"The formal will be held at the Bellavista Function Centre. We plan to hire a band so there will be live music. It should be a wonderful night."

I can feel every capillary in my body frantically trying to pump blood into my heart which has, momentarily, stopped. I have an image of myself standing in the centre of the school, the student body circling me and chanting "Caveman Daddy won't let her go! Caveman Daddy won't let her go!"

The girls start squealing in delight and Amy grabs my arm excitedly.

"What will we wear? Who will we go with? What kind of car? Where will the after-party be?"

I generate as much energy as I can, flash her my most dazzling smile and start to work hard at laying the foundations of enthusiasm early.

"How exciting!" I cry. "I can't wait to find our outfits and do our hair and get some funky jewellery!"

There is no way my dad will let me go.

The flu, an appendix operation, lost house keys – none of

those excuses are going to work this time. I'm going to need to consult encyclopaedias for this one.

From: Ten_Things_I_Hate_About_Me@hotmail.com
To: Rage_Against_The_Machine@hotmail.com
John, I need a lawyer. Can you ask your dad if he'll represent me in my case against my school? I want to sue the board for violating my human rights. And I want to name Mr Anderson in the action and get compensation from him for the psychological trauma I am suffering because of his dumb decision to hold a Year Ten formal at the end of next term.

AS IF I'LL BE ALLOWED!

Shereen went to an all-girls school and that's the only reason she was allowed to go to her formal.

What am I supposed to say when people ask me why I'm not going? I can't use the "my dad won't let me" line. I might as well move to another country.

My reputation will be ruined.

For ever.

Beyond repair.

Gone.

Smashed.

Pulverized.

From: Rage_Against_The_Machine@hotmail.com
To: Ten_Things_I_Hate_About_Me@hotmail.com
Where and when is your formal?

From: Ten_Things_I_Hate_About_Me@hotmail.com
To: Rage_Against_The_Machine@hotmail.com
In June at a reception place in Bellavista. Why do you ask?

From: Rage_Against_The_Machine@hotmail.com
To: Ten_Things_I_Hate_About_Me@hotmail.com
I've got a formal coming up too.

From: Ten_Things_I_Hate_About_Me@hotmail.com
To: Rage_Against_The_Machine@hotmail.com
So then you can understand how desperate my situation is.

From: Rage_Against_The_Machine@hotmail.com
To: Ten_Things_I_Hate_About_Me@hotmail.com
Try and reason with your dad. He let you get a job at Maccas.
I'm sure he'll back down when he realizes how important this
is to you.

But if he does say no, don't stress. It's just a formal. It's no
big deal. People get dressed up and bitch to each other
about who's wearing what and who looks hot and who
doesn't.

I'm sure you can think of a more stimulating way to spend
an evening.

From: Ten_Things_I_Hate_About_Me@hotmail.com
To: Rage_Against_The_Machine@hotmail.com
I will die of a broken heart if he says no.

19

Challenge Peter to a dare and he's up for it faster than a dog to a bone. I've worked it out. He's a bigot and a bully but he's popular because he provides entertainment value. In a nine-to-three world of algebra, chlorophyll and text comprehension, watching Peter put a fart bomb on a teacher's chair or releasing a mouse in home-room is like getting free tickets to a movie.

This morning I overhear him talking to Sam and Chris. Chris says: "I dare you," and Peter answers: "Simple, mate."

Later I'm walking in the corridor when I notice Peter through the door window of a classroom. I stick my nose up close to the window and peer inside for a closer look. In his hand is a tube of superglue. In the other is a whiteboard duster. He catches my gaze and winks. I'm caught off guard and give him a goofy grin.

I turn around and bump into Mr Anderson, who's on corridor patrol. If I walk away, Peter will be caught. If I divert Mr Anderson's attention, Peter just might get away with it.

I'm no snitch. Trying not to look like I have something to hide, I plant myself in front of Mr Anderson and flash him a huge grin.

"Hi sir! How's it going?"

I shouldn't be lurking in the corridor during lunch.

My conversational skills go into fourth gear. He falls for the "I'm a student interested in my teacher's life" routine and we walk down the corridor in deep conversation about his Rottweiler's eating habits.

After lunch we all file into class. Peter takes a seat in the back row, swings on his chair and laughs conspiratorially with Sam and Chris. Fifteen minutes into class Peter raises his hand and asks Mr Anderson to write out the explanation of an algebraic equation on the board. Mr Anderson gets busy on the whiteboard.

It happens halfway between an explanation of why $ax^2 + bx + c = 0$. Mr Anderson grabs the duster and wipes the letter "a" from the board. That small act lands him in trouble.

He quickly realizes that his hand is now partially stuck to a whiteboard duster. He turns around and I estimate that it takes him a mere 2.5 seconds to put two and two together. He is, after all, proficient in algebra.

"Jamie!" It's less than a roar, more than a yell.

"Yes, sir?"

"Am I to believe that it is sheer coincidence that my hand is stuck to this duster and you were lurking behind this classroom door at lunch time today looking, now that I think about it, suspiciously guilty?"

"Yes sir," I mumble. Everybody's eyes are on me.

"Unfortunately for you, I'm not that gullible."

"But I didn't do anything, sir." I don't dare to steal a glance at Peter — that'd be a dead giveaway. Instead I naively wait for him to speak up.

Mr Anderson scans the classroom. "Is there anybody who knows anything about this?" he demands, his face red with rage.

Blank, silent faces and not a peep from Peter.

"Jamie, I'm disappointed in you. This is a very low act."

"I didn't do it, sir!"

"If you didn't do it, then you most certainly know something about it. If it wasn't you, then who was it?"

I hate it when teachers push you into a corner like this. To snitch on Peter would make the rest of my high-school life a tormented hell. I may as well skin myself alive and jump in a bath full of salt. The consequences would be less painful.

I stay silent, defiant. Mr Anderson stares at me. I know he knows I didn't do it. I'm the quiet girl. I've never rocked the boat in class. I'm not the type who would pull off something like this. But in Mr Anderson's world, refusing to expose the perpetrator is equal to committing the act.

I'm stuffed.

"Very well, Jamie. It's your call. I'm going to go to the sickbay to remove this thing from my hand. I'll see you in after-school detention all week and that will be five demerit points in your diary."

A voice sounds from across the room. "You don't have any proof, sir."

"*Excuse me*, Timothy?"

"You're being unfair. You don't have any proof that Jamie did it."

I stare at Timothy in shock.

"This is none of your business!" Mr Anderson cries. "Jamie was outside this classroom door at lunch time and I doubt it was because she was admiring the woodwork on the frames."

"Yeah, but that doesn't prove a thing."

"That's right, sir," I say. "I was just passing through the corridor."

"Rubbish," he says. "You were glued to the door." There is an eruption of giggles.

"This is NOT a laughing matter!"

"It's just that you used the word glued, sir," Timothy says.

"RIGHT! I'll see you in detention after school today too, Timothy."

Timothy shrugs. "Fine."

"I will not have cocky students in my classroom! Open chapter five and complete the entire exercise. Anybody who hasn't finished by the time I return will join Jamie and Timothy this afternoon!"

He turns on his heels and leaves, slamming the door behind him.

"Did you do it?"

"Was it you?"

"It was so cool!"

"It wasn't me," I tell the class.

"So do you know who did it?"

"Nah, I don't."

There are murmurs about my punishment being a travesty of justice and Mr Anderson being an ogre. I look at Peter and he has the audacity to smile and wink at me.

"Thanks for defending me," I say to Timothy.

"No prob. You shouldn't have to take the rap for something you didn't do."

I could swear that he glances at Peter when he says this. Peter doesn't notice. He's too busy laughing victoriously with Chris and Sam.

Peter approaches me after class. "Hey, thanks for not dobbing me in! You're a champ. You know what? You're a really cool chick. A *really* cool chick."

Am I supposed to feel all warm and fuzzy now? The whole situation stinks like garden fertilizer.

Detention is being held in the science lab. That's just an overexcited description for a detached portable classroom planted in the middle of a slab of asphalt next to the staff car park. It's hard to see how the classroom could classify as a laboratory. It basically consists of desks, chairs, a whiteboard, a sink and three gas mains. I hate it when detention is held here because the classroom has no views of the playground and is fairly secluded. You can't wile your time away staring at the guys playing footy or basketball. The only thing worthy of entertainment (and this is getting desperate) is counting the colours of the teachers' cars and trying to work out a statistical equation to explain the dominance of red Ford Falcons.

There are a couple of kids from other classes who are also in trouble for various things: clogging the toilets with tissues, graffiti, getting into a punch-up at the school canteen.

The librarian, Mrs Baxter, is supervising today as Mr Anderson is busy. Now that's power. Punish us with detention but get another teacher to endure the two hours on your behalf. If Mr Anderson was on duty, we wouldn't be allowed to blow our nose without first raising our hand and asking for permission. But Mrs Baxter is on the edge of retiring and isn't really interested in discipline. Everybody's huddled into groups and talking. She's told us she has no problem with us talking as long as we keep our voices down and she can comfortably read her book, *The Passion of Love*.

I steal a glance at Timothy. He looks bored. His head is low and his chin is touching the table. I'm biting my nails and playing with my fringe.

Timothy notices me looking at him and I roll my eyes at Mrs Baxter. He grins at me. Then I lean my chair close to his desk and say: "Thanks again. It was really nice of you to stick up for me."

"I was principle-of-the-matter motivated. I'm not in love with you." His grin is cheeky and I can't help but giggle.

"So what makes you so sure I didn't do it?" I ask.

"A bit of telepathic ability here, a bit of logical deduction there. . ."

"And that led you to work out that it was Peter?"

"How do you know that I know it was Peter?"

"Oh, just a bit of telepathic ability here, a bit of logical deduction there. . ."

You know the saying that the eyes are the window to the soul? Well I think that's crap. I reckon it's not your eyes, it's your smile.

Timothy has a smile on him. Oh yes. He's gone and won a Logie in the smile department. His smile creases the skin around his eyes and sucks up a bit of right cheek into a big, happy dimple.

"He was bragging about it at the lockers," Timothy says. "He's singing your praises too. Of course, he hasn't shown any guilt about the fact that you're in detention. He probably thinks you feel privileged."

I'm ashamed of myself and stare down at the desk.

"So why did you take the blame?"

"Because I'm deeply disturbed. Because I'm craving the approval of a guy who has the brains of ricotta cheese and probably keeps *Mein Kampf* as bedtime reading material."

He bursts out laughing. "Now that's a side of you we don't hear enough."

"Yeah, well, it's reserved for special occasions."

125

"You shouldn't be here."

"What was I supposed to do? Stand up and announce to the world that it was Peter? Do I look like I want a short lifespan?"

"I admit that Mr Anderson was a real arse to put you under that kind of pressure. But you could have taken the rap and then gone up to Peter afterwards and demanded he confess or you'd spill the beans."

I look at him as though he's growing mangoes out of his ears. "You're living in a parallel universe."

He shrugs. "Your universe, or mine – either way he's scum and not worth it."

"It's worth it if I can avoid being known as the resident whistleblower."

He looks at me thoughtfully. "I stuck up for you because I thought that deep down there was a bit of spunk in you, despite the fact that you so obviously try to hide it."

"Sorry to disappoint," I say sarcastically.

"Hey, you don't have to prove yourself to me."

"I wasn't trying to."

"It might get in the way of proving yourself to Peter, right?"

"Hey! That's not fair. You're not under the same sort of pressure as the rest of us *normal* people. You don't care if people find you dorky or weird or stuck-up."

"I'm not worried about other people's adjectives for me."

"Why not?"

"Because if I'm in detention I want to know it was because I did something out of my own free will."

I pretend to find my desk interesting.

"So are you excited about the formal?" I ask.

"It's not really my scene."

"Are you kidding?"

"Everybody standing around with way too much hairspray and gel and aftershave, taking cheesy photos, dancing to a stack of loser songs and generally making an idiot of themselves."

"How about a newsflash: you don't have to be a nonconformist all the time."

"You don't have to be a conformist all the time either."

"You're just conforming to a nonconformist ideology. So you know what? You're a conformist too."

He holds my gaze for a moment and then we burst out laughing.

"I think that's probably enough behavioural analysis for one afternoon, hey?" he says.

"I agree. Let's stick to Gandhi, reality TV and The Worst Of Mr Anderson stories."

20

Bilal comes into my room on Saturday morning and throws himself on to my bed as I'm straightening my hair.

"Why don't you leave it curly?" he asks.

"Because I don't want to knock people over when they walk past me."

"You're such a dag. It looks great curly."

"This is coming from someone with bleached spikes?"

He rolls his eyes at me. "So what are you doing today?"

"I managed to convince Dad to let me go to Amy's house to do *homework*. I had to pretend the visit is linked to my educational enlightenment in order to get permission. So what are you doing?"

"Playing tennis with the boys and then we're off to Home at Darling Harbour. It's Italian night."

I raise my eyebrows at him. "Oh, I see, and that means what? Hot *chicks*?"

He grins and nods his head. "Oh yeah, that's for sure. Plus the music goes off!"

"Like you could pick up anyway," I say, throwing my brush at him. "And I suppose you'll be home at four in the morning and give Dad a heart attack?"

"I get so sick of him bossing me around. I'm eighteen years old. When's he going to let me be a man and make my own decisions about my life?"

I snort. "What decisions are they? Clubbing? Drinking? Very impressive, Bilal."

He rolls his eyes again and leans back against my bedhead, his hands behind his head.

"OK, I don't expect the green light from him about my social life. And I know it's wrong in Islam, blah, blah, blah. But do you know what annoys me most, Jam?"

"What?"

"Dad still carries on about me being a dropout. So I didn't inherit his brains. I just don't have that academic side to me. I've never been good at school. I'm good with my hands. Engines, I understand. Trigonometry, Shakespeare, all that stuff goes into my head and comes out as fairy floss."

"I know what you mean. He has these high expectations for all of us. But he sets them without consulting us or thinking about what we want or how we feel."

"Sometimes I feel like telling him to go jump."

"Tell Dad to go jump?" I look at him incredulously. "Do you think this is an episode of *Neighbours* or something? Don't you remember the taste of Dove soap? Remember the time you came home from school and Dad told you to clean your room or you wouldn't be allowed to go to your basketball game? I distinctly remember what you said: *Do you want a knuckle sandwich, old man?*"

He slowly breaks out into a grin as he remembers the incident. "I didn't realize what it meant! I was a kid! Man, that soap killed me! I was burping soapsuds for days!"

"You could have stacked a dishwasher in your mouth, that's how sparkling clean it was."

We collapse into giggles.

"So telling Dad to go jump isn't really advisable."

He laughs. "I'm not that stupid. But it still pisses me off though. I want to be a mechanic and he gives me no respect for that."

"Things would have been different if Mum was alive."

He sighs. "She would have understood."

I give him a sly grin. "But she would have roasted you alive if she knew you drink and go out with girls!"

"I would have given anything up for her," he says softly. "I miss her like crazy."

"Me too."

"Dad just doesn't understand me. He wants us all to be *professionals*. He's the one who's been behind a taxi wheel for years. If he regrets not using his PhD he shouldn't take it out on us. That's just hypocriticism!"

"The word is hypocritical, Bilal. Maybe Dad does have a point about you dropping out."

He lunges forward and puts me in a headlock. I laugh and splutter, begging him to release me.

"Say that I'm the best-looking, most intelligent guy in the world!" he says.

"Let me go, you idiot!" I cry.

He keeps me down, grinning in my face. "Say it, Jam!"

"OK, OK, you're the best."

He releases me and we burst out laughing.

Today is the first time I have visited Amy. It feels strange because I'm not used to seeing her outside of school. When I arrive I feel slightly awkward. I sit on the edge of the couch wondering if we'll run out of things to say to each other. With so many topics off limits, I wonder what's left to talk about. I seem to constantly hide behind the superficial with Amy. I can discuss movies, celebrities, music, but I can't talk about what's really going on in my life.

Amy has a bowl of popcorn ready and packets of crisps and chocolate.

"I borrowed *The Ring*," she says. "I've heard it's really scary."

"That sounds great," I say as I stuff my mouth with a handful of popcorn.

We're watching the movie when Amy's mother walks into the room. "Hello," she says.

"Hi, I'm Jamie," I say.

"Yes, I know," she says, smiling at me. "Amy's told me all about you."

I almost want to let out a hoot. There wouldn't exactly be much to say.

We chat for a couple of minutes and then she turns to Amy. "Is your father having dinner here tonight?"

"How am I supposed to know?" Amy says tensely, staring at the television screen.

"Well, can you please go and ask him. He's in the study."

I steal a glance at Amy and notice the mortified expression on her face. I pretend to be oblivious to their conversation and concentrate on extracting a popcorn kernel that's stuck in my teeth.

"Why can't you ask him yourself?"

Amy's mother gives her a stern look. "Amy, I am not in the mood for this conversation. You know very well why I'm not going into that study."

Amy lets out an exaggerated sigh.

"Fine!" Amy's mother cries and storms out of the room.

I don't want to intrude but I can't pretend that nothing is wrong either. So I tread delicately. "Is everything OK?" I ask her gently.

She looks at me and in a huffy voice says: "I really don't want to talk about it, if you don't mind."

She's throwing my words back in my face. They sting like a paper cut.

"I didn't mean to shut you out before," I say slowly.

"That's fine. And I don't mean to shut you out now."

I fumble with my skirt, averting my eyes from her gaze.

"Your door is closed and so is mine. Let's just leave it at that."

My throat is burning with the anticipation of tears. But I swallow hard and manage to control myself.

I catch the bus before it gets dark and meet Shereen at a café in Parramatta, where she had spent the afternoon with her friends. I didn't want Shereen to pick me up from Amy's house, all dressed up in her Yin Yang hijab.

"It was awesome, Jamilah," she says as we're driving home. "We really made progress. We're organizing a petition to protest against the torture of Falun Gong practitioners in China. A Chinese diplomat is visiting Sydney next week and we plan to work with a local human-rights group and hold a massive vigil in the centre of the city. You should come along."

"Sorry, I think I'm getting a massage with a chainsaw that day. Maybe next time."

She rolls her eyes at me. "Don't be such a bimbo."

"I don't know how you have the energy. All that protesting makes no difference whatsoever. The world still sucks. It doesn't matter how loud you scream or how big your placards are."

"Don't be so cynical, Jamilah. We can make a difference."

"The last time I checked, the war in Iraq is still going, prisoners are being abused, asylum seekers are still getting locked up, Indigenous Australians are dying in prison and African children are still starving. Effective track record."

"Silence is consent, Jamilah!"

"I know you're passionate, Shereen, and I can't believe I'm going to admit this, but Dad has a point. If you want to do something about all the injustice, do something that works."

She purses her lips and grips the steering wheel. "None of you understand. Don't you care about anything besides watching TV?"

"As a matter of fact, yes I do." I turn my body towards her and give her an intense look.

"Why are you looking at me like that?"

"I need help. I need to draw on your infinite wisdom. I need to rely on your expertise and brilliance and—"

She chuckles. "Enough already, what do you want?"

"I need you to help me persuade Dad to let me go to my Year Ten formal. It's the most important event of the year. And if I don't go I will personally ring Kofi Annan and tell him that you refused to provide humanitarian assistance to a person in desperate need."

She bursts out laughing. "You need the entire United Nations to help you convince Dad."

I slam my head against the dashboard. "I have to go, Shereen! I'll be the only one left out. My class is planning the whole night. Dresses, hair, cars, where they'll go afterwards. It will be the topic on everybody's lips for the next two years. I will be excluded from the private jokes and 'do you remember what happened when' stories. My life will be OVER."

"Note to Jamilah: Do not overreact."

"Note to Miss-Goody-Two-Shoes-I-Pray-Five-Times-A-Day: I reckon Allah would be pretty unimpressed if you ignored the desperate plea of a family member – of your own sister!"

"Look, Jamilah, I'll try my best but I don't hold much hope that he'll let you. He's not dumb. He knows what goes on at these things. He'll hear the word 'formal' and think of all those Hollywood 'I lost my virginity at my prom night' movies."

I groan. "Tell me about it! Look Miss Tree-Hugger, just try. Please."

She glances sidelong at me and scrunches up her nose. "Tree-hugger? Do you think I hug trees?"

I grin at her. "No. I think you're way more wacko than that. Hugging is mild. You probably talk to them and celebrate their birthdays too."

She takes one hand off the steering wheel and pinches me playfully in the side. "How on earth are we related?"

"See? All that hippie stuff has made you forget the birds and the bees. You see, one day Mum and Dad conceived you and then. . ."

She shudders and yells out to me to shut up.

"So you'll talk to him?"

She looks at me and then nods.

"You're not so bad after all!"

Shereen peeks her head around my door later that evening.

"I tried."

"And?"

She casts her eyes down. "Sorry, Jam."

21

You might as well hook me on to a fishing line and throw me into the harbour. My life is well and truly over.

Miss Sajda rushes into our classroom at madrasa this evening, her face exploding into a wide grin. Mustafa, Samira, Hasan and I are sitting around a table. They've been telling me about a CD of rap "ballads" titled *Whassup With That?* which they have produced. They say "produced" as though they've struck a record deal, when all they did was hang out at a café in Leichhardt writing out a rap song about racism, pride and baggy hipster jeans on loose napkins.

"Whassup, Miss Sajda?" Mustafa asks.

"Your band is wanted!"

"Where?"

"Who?"

"No way!"

We sit up in our seats, fidgeting with excited anticipation as we wait for her response.

"I sent out pamphlets about the band to all the local schools. Guildford High is holding their Year Ten formal in June and they want to hire a band with, and I quote, "Middle Eastern music". Apparently the teachers have noticed quite a bit of racial tension amongst some of the students and feel that they need a reminder about the importance of multiculturalism. Isn't it fantastic?"

It's all I can do to stop myself from passing out.

"Did you say Guildford High?" I whisper in a strained voice.

She nods but then, noticing my pale face, says: "Is something wrong, Jamilah?"

I gulp down hard. "That's my school. And my formal."

"Wow! What a nice coincidence!" Samira says.

"You'll be famous!" Hasan says. "That's so cool."

"It's a disaster," I say.

"Why?" Miss Sajda asks.

I slump down into my chair and groan, hiding my face in my hands. "An absolute disaster," I repeat miserably.

Mustafa sits up in his chair. "It's an amazing

opportunity, Jamilah! Don't tell me you're going to back out? Are you worried about your dad? I'm sure he'll agree. It's your formal. You're going anyway, so what's the big deal?"

I let out a short, cynical laugh. "Who said I'm going?"

"Oh," he says quietly.

"Would you like me to talk to him?" Miss Sajda asks.

I look up at her. "No thanks. I'm going to have to fight for this on my own."

I arrive home from madrasa and find my dad watching the news. I sit next to him.

"How was madrasa?"

"Great."

"You're enjoying playing in the band, aren't you?"

"I love it. We're good too. You'd be proud of us."

"That's my girl. Maybe you'll get to perform at some weddings or the Arabic Festival. But only once in a while. I don't want it to become a regular thing."

"Speaking of performing, Dad," I venture, my voice shaking slightly, "we've already received our first offer."

He turns down the volume on the television and looks at me with delight. "Really? That's wonderful. Where?"

"Actually, Dad," I stammer, "it's the strangest coincidence. My Year Ten formal is being held in June and the teachers have requested that our band perform."

"Formal?"

"Yes, my formal." I nervously clear my throat.

He leans back in his chair and sighs. "Ahh, the one you sent Shereen to talk to me about."

I avert my eyes. "Can I go?"

"Is it mixed?"

"What do you mean?"

"Mixed between boys and girls?"

"Well, yes, the male gender will be present."

"I won't allow it, Jamilah."

"But Dad! Everyone's going!"

"Jamilah, we're different. These formals are not proper environments for respectable girls and boys. There will be alcohol, dancing."

"Of course they won't serve alcohol."

"I'm sure the kids will somehow manage to get their hands on alcohol either before or after the party. Jamilah, dating and dancing with boys are not for you."

"I'll be the biggest loser in my class."

"Only if you allow people to think that you feel deprived. If you're proud of your beliefs then nobody will dare to say anything. People are guided by your attitude. You need to learn that."

"Can't you just back down for once? Please, Dad? How can I let the band down? They're all so excited!"

"Look, Jamilah, I have certain principles and rules and I won't compromise on them. For you to go to the formal is out of the question. I do not trust these sorts of events. As for the band, I'll let you play with them but you have to leave when they leave."

"But Dad!"

"Enough, Jamilah!" he cries. "All you do is argue with me! Why can't you ever respect my will?"

"Why can't you ever give any consideration to mine?" I run to my room, throw myself on to my bed and burst into tears.

22

Ever since the day Mr Anderson opened his big fat mouth about the formal and threw my life into a meat grinder, my class has been acting like we've been offered tickets to the Oscars. I can't count how many times I've had to pretend to enjoy participating in heated discussions about whether a limo is sexier than a BMW; where the after-party should be held and who will supply the grog; and, most importantly, who will be our dates.

Until now, I'm quite confident that nobody suspects that while the rest of my class will be dancing to a funk remix and maxing out their digital camera capacity, I will be at home glued to my computer desk, ferociously taking my anger out on my keyboard as I bore John to death with my sad, pathetic existence.

In home-room this morning Mr Anderson drops the bombshell about an "ethnic band" being hired to play at the formal.

"They're an up-and-coming young local group, all of Middle Eastern background. It should be a lovely treat for you all."

Peter snorts out loud. "Middle Eastern music? I thought the formal was supposed to be fun."

My heart starts thumping in my chest.

"It's hard to appreciate good music when your head is full of sawdust," Ahmed says.

"Oh, do you have time to be a music critic in between making bombs?"

Ahmed stands up. "Why don't you come here and say that to my face?"

"That's enough!" Mr Anderson cries. "Both of you keep your mouth shut."

"He started it!" Ahmed yells. "He's a racist pig!"

"Who are you calling a pig, you dumb Leb?"

"Right! I'll see both of you in detention at lunch time. Let this be a lesson to you all. I will NOT accept such conduct in my classroom."

There are murmurs of "how unfair", "he started it", "uncalled for". Mr Anderson flashes the class a devastatingly chilling look and everybody stops talking.

*

"An *ethnic* band?" Liz says, a weird look on her face. "I wonder what that will be like."

"So what?" Amy says. "I don't know what the big deal is. As long as we get to dress up I couldn't care less what music there is."

"Yeah, but what if it's all belly-dancing music?" Liz scrunches her face up. "I wouldn't have a clue!"

I can't take this. "I've got to go!" I rush off and bump into Ahmed on my way to the bathroom. His fists are clenched tight and he looks furious.

"You were there, Jamie. Do you think I deserve detention?"

"Not at all," I say.

"Peter is the biggest jerk and I get the same punishment as him. It's so unfair."

"Mr Anderson was probably just trying to make a point about speaking aloud in class," I say lightly. "You know how he is when it comes to not putting our hands up ... I'm *joking*," I say as I see he's still scowling.

"It's not a joking matter. Just because I refuse to put up with Peter's prejudice, I get punished. I'm not going to apologize for my background."

"But you know he gives you a hard time about it, so why can't you just ignore him?"

His eyes widen in disbelief. "Ignore him? No way! I was born here and I deserve the same respect he demands. I'm not going to be made to feel like I'm some tourist without a visa who needs to be thrown out of the country. You wouldn't understand what it feels like to be constantly treated like a negotiable citizen."

How wrong he is. And how lucky. The same prejudice and bigotry that silences me, vocalizes him. And even though my silence protects me, I'm the one walking with my head down.

The bell rings after science the next day and I'm packing my books away, listening to Peter tell me about his new PlayStation, when Timothy walks up beside my desk and stands there, waiting patiently for me to finish. We've arranged to meet up to do some internet research at the library for our Gandhi assignment. Peter stops talking and looks Timothy up and down.

"What do you want?" Peter asks in a surprised tone.

"Nothing," Timothy answers. "Just waiting for Jamie."

Peter looks at me incredulously. "Is something going. . .?"

I give him a mortified look and quickly correct him. "No, no! Nothing like that. Of course not!" I say it so vehemently and quickly that I don't have time to think about the consequences. But it's too late anyway: the damage has been done. Timothy raises his eyebrows at me and walks off.

OK I'll admit it. I'll admit that I don't have the guts to run after him. I am officially walking around without a spinal chord. Peter turns back to me and chuckles.

"Ha! You crushed the goldfish, you ice queen."

"We're working on our history assignment. . ." And then, for a single moment, a touch of courage rises within me. "He's not such a bad guy, you know."

"Do you have the hots for him or something?"

"No."

He looks at me closely. "Yeah, you don't look like the type who has bad taste."

The courage falls away. I look down at my hands, feeling like I'm betraying Timothy.

"You know what's nice about you, Jamie? What makes you different to the other chicks in this class?"

"What?"

"You've got no confidence in yourself."

"*Huh?*"

"You're so shy and awkward and quiet. It's such a refreshing change to all the chicks who are so *out there*." He rolls his eyes. "All they do is whine about guys not respecting them and taking them seriously. They're always out to prove themselves. They want to be defined. You, on the other hand, seem happy just floating along. You have no idea how cool that is." He flashes me a large smile and walks out of the room.

I walk slowly to the library. *No confidence. Shy and awkward. Floating along.* I've attracted the attention of Peter Clarkson for all the wrong reasons. Although I've tried so hard to hide my identity, I never imagined I had reduced myself to a passive, mute *chick*.

Timothy is sitting at a computer. He has his Discman on

146

and is tapping his foot to the music. I approach him cautiously and sit down beside him.

"Sorry about before . . . I didn't mean to . . . I hope you're not hurt."

"You've got to care in the first place to get hurt."

I'm taken aback and look down at my hands. "That's not a very nice thing to say."

He clears his throat and swings back on his chair. "I meant I don't care about *Peter*."

"Oh."

"It's obvious you do, though."

"What?"

"And I find that surprising."

"Hey, you don't know me well enough to judge me."

He stares at me. "Fair enough." He pauses. "But I do know that you're not part of his cheerleading squad every time he decides to mouth somebody off. You're an uncomfortable spectator. Am I right?"

"That's pretty presumptuous of you."

"So I'm wrong?"

"Well, no. Yes. I mean, that's not the point!"

"Look, sorry, I can see this bothers you. Let's talk about something else."

"OK, how about we turn the microscope around on you? Why don't you care what people think about you? That's not normal. Actually, it's quite arrogant. You're not such an amazing person that you can avoid putting in some effort into attracting people!"

"Relax. I understand the whole 'no man's an island' thing. Certain people's opinions I care about. If I respect somebody then of course I want their approval. But I'm not going to be a phoney in order to score brownie points with somebody I don't respect. I'm selective. That's the difference."

"Well, *sorry*, I'm not as brave and strong as you. Why don't you just bottle yourself and market yourself at a Myer perfume counter? One spray and we can all be as cool and confident as Timothy!"

"Hey, relax, I'm not judging you."

"You're not *judging* me? You do it so well you could be eligible for a Supreme Court appointment!"

He gives me an apologetic look. "Sorry if that's the way I've come across."

I look at him closely and then half smile. "It's OK. I have a lot to be sorry for too."

23

From: Rage_Against_The_Machine@hotmail.com
To: Ten_Things_I_Hate_About_Me@hotmail.com
My dad and I were supposed to spend the weekend together. Yet he still managed to book himself out for the whole weekend. His itinerary:

Friday night: Law Society dinner

Saturday morning: Sleep in and get over a hangover

Saturday: Lunch with some of his work colleagues on an all-day harbour cruise

Sunday morning/afternoon: Sleep in and get over a hangover

Sunday night: Cocktail function

NB: Children under 18 not allowed.
NB: Children over 55 allowed.

I felt like the ad breaks in his weekend. The only time he had available for me was when we crossed paths in the hallway or in the hour he had to get ready before leaving. He would call me to his room. I would sit on the edge of the bed and watch him as he put on his designer tie/designer polo shirt/designer socks.

You know something, Jamilah? Without fail he manages to get under my skin. Right under the fatty and muscle layers. He is only capable of communicating with me by lecturing me about my lack of ambition and my "pathetic resistance" to his dream of me following in his footsteps and becoming a lawyer in his firm.

Boy does he piss me off.

From: Ten_Things_I_Hate_About_Me@hotmail.com
To: Rage_Against_The_Machine@hotmail.com
So your dad wants you to be a lawyer? What's wrong with that? Everybody's always so cynical about the legal profession, but they're not such a bad lot, are they? I'm sure they also give their seats up to pregnant women on trains and don't take a sherbet lolly from the Spastic Society box without dropping thirty cents in.

From: Rage_Against_The_Machine@hotmail.com
To: Ten_Things_I_Hate_About_Me@hotmail.com

I have nothing against lawyers *per se* (that's lawyer lingo my dad taught me through example: "*You are not stupid*, per se"; "*I am not drunk*, per se"). Mum is a lawyer too. She works for legal aid. Don't go *ahhh* on me. It's not as romantic or righteous as you may think. There are times she comes home from work swearing about "bloody greedy plaintiffs" and "arsehole insurers". She started idealistic and is probably now worn out.

But I still think she believes in it. If I've learnt anything from her, it's that you have to believe in what you're doing or you might as well find employment picking up dog poo from park gardens.

From: Ten_Things_I_Hate_About_Me@hotmail.com
To: Rage_Against_The_Machine@hotmail.com
So what's the objection to law?

From: Rage_Against_The_Machine@hotmail.com
To: Ten_Things_I_Hate_About_Me@hotmail.com
It's not an objection to law. It's an objection to my dad's legal path. He wants me to be in a law firm where the size of your office, the extent of your stationery drawer, and the direction your window faces are as important as the quality of your work.

He quit his last firm because he didn't feel respected. Note: He was a partner. He had a car space which, on an annual basis, costs the same as an average house mortgage. But he didn't have a harbour view. That counted as a "lack of respect" because at his firm having a harbour view was the definitive indication that you had MADE IT.

Now that basically comes with a lot of arse-kissing and lower-back issues from sitting at a computer for an unholy amount of time each day. Not to mention having a house you treat as a hotel and a family you treat as hotel staff (I was the concierge).

From: Ten_Things_I_Hate_About_Me@hotmail.com
To: Rage_Against_The_Machine@hotmail.com
I don't think my dad believes in what he does. What's there to believe in when you're a taxi driver? *I believe in providing a quality transport experience to commuters and I believe that they have the right to travel through Sydney's streets with respect and dignity and air conditioning and low volume radio?*

Maybe some people don't have the luxury to plan their careers according to their beliefs.

From: Rage_Against_The_Machine@hotmail.com
To: Ten_Things_I_Hate_About_Me@hotmail.com
Do you have a boyfriend?

From: Ten_Things_I_Hate_About_Me@hotmail.com
To: Rage_Against_The_Machine@hotmail.com
No. Anyway, I'd be dead meat if my dad ever found out.

From: Rage_Against_The_Machine@hotmail.com
To: Ten_Things_I_Hate_About_Me@hotmail.com
Are you serious? Like those honour killings you hear about?

From: Ten_Things_I_Hate_About_Me@hotmail.com
To: Rage_Against_The_Machine@hotmail.com
No, you space cadet. Sheez, this is why I hate opening up to people about my family! Can't I be metaphorical without having my dad equated to a Taliban war lord?

From: Rage_Against_The_Machine@hotmail.com
To: Ten_Things_I_Hate_About_Me@hotmail.com
Deep breaths. Think nice thoughts. A bunch of red roses. Chocolate with hazelnut centres. You can do this. You can *calm down*. Just focus.

From: Ten_Things_I_Hate_About_Me@hotmail.com
To: Rage_Against_The_Machine@hotmail.com
If I didn't like you so much I'd be a smart-arse to you for that. So do you have a girlfriend?

From: Rage_Against_The_Machine@hotmail.com
To: Ten_Things_I_Hate_About_Me@hotmail.com
We broke up. We didn't have much in common. I couldn't talk to her. Sometimes you just want somebody to laugh with and open up to.

From: Ten_Things_I_Hate_About_Me@hotmail.com
To: Rage_Against_The_Machine@hotmail.com
Tell me about it.

From: Rage_Against_The_Machine@hotmail.com
To: Ten_Things_I_Hate_About_Me@hotmail.com
I have to go, Jamilah. My mum needs help opening a can of tuna. She can defend an armed robber in a court of law but she has difficulties working out a can-opener.

24

I step out of the house this morning to catch the bus to school. It's the beginning of April and the autumn breeze is sweet and warm and puts a smile on my face. There is a direct correlation between the weather and my moods. That's just the type of person I am. When it's hot and sticky and I'm trying to survive Sydney's notorious summer humidity, I am grumpy and irritable until somebody throws me into a swimming pool. When the sky is overcast and gloomy there aren't enough jam-centred Krispy Kreme doughnuts in the world to pick me up. I thrive on sunny days and the smell of freshly cut grass and the scent of jasmine bushes. That probably explains why my dad and I fight more in winter than we do in spring. Actually, that probably has more to do with the fact that there's no daylight saving in winter, so my sunset curfew is pushed forward and I generally have to be home before Larry Emdur has had a chance to introduce the contestants on *The Price Is Right*.

How sad.

It's the end of term one break and as I walk to the bus stop enjoying the rays of sun hug and tickle my body, I find myself wondering whether I have been overreacting to not being allowed to go to the formal.

Then again, this is high school. The system is designed to sort out the cool from the uncool, the strong from the weak, the smart from the dumb. We're not protected by political correctness or common decency in high school. If you're a guy and you're not so good at shooting hoops or kicking a footy, you're a faggot. Nobody even flickers an eyelash. If you're a girl who doesn't go out with guys and has never been kissed, you're either frigid or a lezo. If you get good marks and know how to string an essay together, you're a nerd.

So if your dad doesn't let you go to the formal, where does that leave you?

Am I overreacting? Who am I kidding? I've been way too relaxed about this until now.

So I find the time during class to write a letter to my dad. When I go home that night I proofread it and fiddle with it until I feel it's just right. I wait for him to go to sleep and then leave it in an envelope on the jar of coffee for him to read in the morning.

It goes like this:

Dear Dad/Baba/The Man I Look Up To In My Life,
I have it on good authority that you were young once. I know I tell you that I don't believe it and that Tete gave birth to an ancient fossil, but that's just a joke, OK? I really do appreciate that you, too, were a teenager a long, long time ago and also knew what it felt like to want to fit in with your fellow colleagues in the student body of the educational establishment at which you were sent to learn and grow by your parents.

Well, DITTO (that means "same here" in case you've forgotten the line in the movie Ghost starring Demi Moore and Patrick Swayze, the guy you think looks like Uncle Hisham, which I've never quite understood but, well, everyone's entitled to their own opinion).

I am nearly sixteen years old and very VERY responsible and reliable and mature and trustworthy with good morals and strong beliefs. I am learning in debating at school that every ~~prepo proposition~~ statement should be backed up with an example, so I shall provide you with some examples in support of my very VERY convincing argument.

1. *I have never been suspended or expelled from school.*
2. *I always return DVDs to the store on time.*
3. *I rarely lose my house keys.*
4. *I always buy a train ticket even when I know I'm going to a station where there are no inspectors.*
5. *I cry at all the Quit Smoking commercials and happy to say that they have deterred me.*

6. *I also cry at all the "If you drink then drive you're a bloody idiot" commercials and am happy to say that I have never, and will never, enter a car with a driver who is over the limit.*

7. *Or has had any alcohol at all.*

8. *Or may have contemplated having alcohol and getting behind the wheel.*

9. *I am completely opposed to premarital relationships and always refrain from any flirtatious or suggestive conversations with the opposite sex to protect my modesty. I try not to laugh at boys' jokes because it might encourage them and send them the wrong message. I am conscious of how I behave in front of boys and always make sure to wear a Bonds singlet underneath my thick top during PE.*

10. *I enjoy madrasa heaps and heaps. I am grateful to have the opportunity to be bilingual.*

Those are only a small number of examples, Dad. Please consider them. Please let me go to my formal. If you refuse I will never know happiness or joy or popularity at school again. This could affect my academic performance and mean I end up failing my subjects and never gaining the marks or confidence to get a high score and a PhD in your footsteps.

So PLEASE let me go to my formal.

PLEASE.

Sincerely Jamilah

Who inherited your eyes but not your nose (thank God, hey?! haha)
XXXXXXXXXXXXXXXXXXXXXXXXXXXXXXOOOOOOOO
OOOOOOOOOOOOOOOOOO

I receive three text messages from my dad during school the next day. I'm impressed. He isn't the best when it comes to sending texts. I allow myself to believe, for a fleeting moment, that if he's put in the effort he must have good news.

My heart pounds as I open each one.

Text message 1: *Th2nk you for yor swit letTTer Jamilah. I will kipe it alwAyS. But the answa IS*

Linked text message 2: *sTill no. You wil understand one da*

Linked text message 3: *Y*

And that's it. For a measly seventy-five cents my father has officially sealed my fate and declared my life well and truly over.

25

From: Ten_Things_I_Hate_About_Me@hotmail.com
To: Rage_Against_The_Machine@hotmail.com
Here are the latest developments in my life.

I'm not allowed to go to the formal.

The band I play in at madrasa has been hired to perform.

My dad says I can play in the band but I'll have to leave early.

Here's the thing, John.

If I leave early I'll be a loser.

If I play in the band I'll be exposing myself. Off comes the disguise. In comes the girl who hid her identity behind a web of lies and deceit.

I have now seriously developed catagelophobia (fear of being ridiculed) and allodoxaphobia (fear of opinions). I

160

need professional help. Alternatively, I could do with some catastrophic weather conditions on the date of the formal leading to its cancellation.

From: Rage_Against_The_Machine@hotmail.com
To: Ten_Things_I_Hate_About_Me@hotmail.com
Jamilah/She Who Holds Two Names: I learned something on Google today. It is impossible to lick your elbow, and 23% of all photocopier faults worldwide are caused by people sitting on them and photocopying their butts.

Why am I telling you this?

Because you should be exerting your efforts and energy into surfing the net to arm yourself with useless but interesting information, NOT spending your time nurturing your catagelophobia. You need an antidote. I've been in the lab and boiled one up for you.

ANTIDOTE TO CATAGELOPHOBIA
Also works for allodoxaphobia and other fear-of-what-people-might-say/think related conditions

You need to stop worrying about how other people judge you.

You need to trust that your friends will respect you for who you are. → But they'll never do that If you don't respect yourself first.

It's clear that you don't respect yourself and that is disturbing because you are poetry + music + funny + caring = worth it (and that's not only in the L'Oreal hair dye commercial kind of way).

You need to know that there are more than ten things you should LOVE (or at least like – small steps) about yourself.

If you take one thing out of our emails, take that.

From: Ten_Things_I_Hate_About_Me@hotmail.com
To: Rage_Against_The_Machine@hotmail.com
I wish friends like you came in person.

I've been working at McDonald's for several weeks now, Mondays and Wednesdays, and loving every minute of it. I know it's just a casual job. That it's no big deal in the wider scheme of things. I'm basically serving fries and burgers, scrubbing disgusting oil marks out of appliances, mopping floors and stacking serviettes.

But it's a small taste of independence and I'm happy to scrape solidified lard out of a chips machine if it means extending my curfew, earning my own money and having some time outside the house.

I'm on my half-hour break. I'm sitting outside with a drink and burger when I feel a tap on my shoulder. I turn around and am startled to see Timothy grinning down at me.

"Great uniform," he says, looking me up and down.

"Attractive isn't it. . . What are you doing here?"

He props himself up on the table so that his legs are dangling beside mine, looks at me and shrugs his shoulders. "My grandma's cooking dinner tonight. Chops and mash. She undercooks the chops. I can't stand that. I like my meat to make a thud if it were to hit the ground. So I thought I'd go for the healthier alternative. I only live a couple of blocks away."

I laugh. "Why don't you just get off your butt and cook the chops yourself? That way you can overcook them the way you want."

"That would take effort. I'm not into effort."

"My sympathies."

"Thanks."

"To your *grandma*."

He chuckles. "Smart-arse."

"Very polite."

"Politeness is just a fake front for people who don't have the guts to speak their mind."

I laugh. "Oh Timothy, that's just so contrived. Are you trying to be philosophical or something?"

"I figure if I say something profound, I'll earn myself a free packet of nuggets." He smiles. "So you live around here too?"

"Yeah, about ten minutes away. You live with your grandma, right?"

"Yeah. And my mum."

"So why'd you move from the North Shore to Guildford? If you don't mind me asking."

"My parents divorced." He suddenly seems distracted and jumps off the table. "Well, I'm off to get some food," he says, taking out his wallet. "Enjoy your break. I'll catch you at school tomorrow."

When I get home tonight I email John.

From: Ten_Things_I_Hate_About_Me@hotmail.com
To: Rage_Against_The_Machine@hotmail.com
The strangest thing happened today. One of the guys in my class came to my work. And I have no idea why. Have I ever told you about Timothy?

I receive an email back. Only it tells me that John has blocked me from his email account. Yes. That's right. Blocked me. He has officially told me to piss off in cyber language. Why? What on earth have I done to deserve being equated to spam mail? Maybe I bored him to death. All that ID talk and baklava background sent him mad. Whatever the reason, all I want to know is one thing: just who can I count as a friend now?

26

"**W**hat do you mean you don't want to play?"

Mustafa is pacing up and down in front of me, hands flying, trying to come to terms with my announcement that I don't want to play at my formal. Samira and Hasan are sitting on their desks, staring at me in disbelief.

"My dad won't let me go. If I play in the band, I can't stay. I have to leave with you guys. It's just too humiliating."

"If admitting that you have to leave early is freaking you out so much, make something up!" Samira says. "Tell your friends that you've got to get home early because there's a gas leak!"

"If I play in the band there will be consequences for me."

"Like what, man?" Hasan asks.

"Yeah, like what?" Mustafa asks.

"It's long and complicated and moronic. It's gotten completely out of hand. Even if I wanted to change things, I couldn't do it without stuffing things up between me and my friends. Let alone the rest of my class."

Mustafa stands in front of me and stares at me closely. "What are you talking about? You're not making any sense."

I sigh. "Look, don't worry about the details. I'm not in. You can still play without me."

I don't let them argue with me.

"Can I persuade you to change your mind?"

"Nope. Sorry Miss Sajda."

She cups her chin in her hand and leans on the desk. "What are you afraid of?"

I take a slow breath. "You wouldn't understand."

"Do you think I came to this country wrapping myself in the Lebanese flag and proudly walking down the street?"

"Well, yeah. You always seem so comfortable with being Lebanese."

"It's been a long struggle to accept myself, Jamilah. I'll tell you something. I migrated to Sydney with my ex-husband when I was twenty-seven years old. Saed would come home from work depressed. People called him names, teased his accent, put down his religion. He was desperate to fit in as an Australian. So he disconnected us from family and community. He insisted that we imitate, not integrate. I was cut off from a support network. Every night Saed would go to the local pub with his workmates. Having a beer with them made him Aussie, he thought. We no longer ate dinner together. That used to be a sacred ritual for us back home. He came home tipsy, sometimes drunk. He lost the respect of Lebanese-Australians *and* Anglo-Australians, the people he tried so hard to impress. He thought he had made true friends. But I know they ridiculed him behind his back. So he gained nothing."

She stops and her face is suddenly animated. She rubs her hands together, grinning wildly at me. "Big family dinners and a million conversations around the dinner table! Thick Arabic *ahwa* boiled on a coal barbecue and drunk with syrupy baklava and *konefa*. Drinking it over stories about back home when we played on snow-capped mountains after school and spent our weekends swimming in the Mediterranean. Picking *warak ayneb* from the pot while nobody's looking and scooping humous into fresh loaves of bread and letting it melt in your mouth! The *darabuka* and *oud* and *tabla* hypnotizing your hips into dancing around the lounge room with your cousins and aunts. A community of aunts and uncles and cousins, even when they're not blood relations."

I giggle. "Sounds familiar."

"But wait, Jamilah. Look closer. The family dinner is in the backyard of your suburban Sydney home. The Arabic coffee is being boiled over a barbecue you bought from Bunnings. The *warak ayneb* is home-grown and the humous is from the local supermarket. The boys and girls experiment with their parents' instruments while *Neighbours* is on in the background. That's *your* Australian landscape, Jamilah."

"Even so, I can't let it spill beyond my driveway. Because no matter how much I love it, what does it have to do with reality?"

"It's *your* reality!"

"But out there, in the real world, at train stations and on talkback radio and on the streets and in the shops, I've only ever felt that my heritage is something to be ashamed of."

"How can you say that, Jamilah?"

"How can I not? You remember, don't you? When those teenage boys gang-raped girls in Sydney, it was the boys' Lebanese-Muslim background that was put on trial. I went to school and I watched Peter Clarkson cross-examine Ahmed for a crime he did not commit. I read headlines describing the crimes as 'Middle Eastern rape'. I've never heard of Anglo burglary or Caucasian murder. If an Anglo-Australian commits a crime, the only descriptions we get are the colour of his clothes and hair."

"I know, Jamilah. And it angers me too. But I won't give in."

She doesn't realize that I already have. I remember too well the way kids would tease me in primary school when my mum packed me Lebanese bread and *labne* for lunch. I see how people respond to Shereen when she walks around wearing her hijab. Like she might have a bomb hitched under her skirt.

I remember my mum trying to fit in with the other

168

mothers at my primary school. It was the Grade Five food fair and my mum came along to the mothers' meeting and made arrangements to cook something for me to contribute. My mum slaved in the kitchen for a day, making trays of traditional Lebanese food. I brought it along to share with the class and the kids just laughed at me. They had their Vegemite and cheese sandwiches and chocolate crackles and fairy bread. I had kebabs and kofta and tabouli and pastries. Some of the other mothers laughed. I could smell their condescension. It smacked my nose like milk gone sour.

When there's so much fear and misunderstanding and ridicule, why would anybody want to stand out? As well-meaning as Miss Sajda's efforts may be, I'm not interested in being a hybrid identity. I've learned that the safest thing is to leave the kebabs at home and stick to fairy bread and Vegemite.

27

Today I'm at work, out the back in the food preparation area attending to the spillages, when one of my dad's family friends, Uncle Joseph, walks up to the counter and spots me as he places his order.

"Jamilah?" he cries out in surprise.

I want to duck. Uncle Joseph is one of those people I would like to see buried in a time capsule out in the Sahara desert with instructions that the capsule be opened in the year 2090. That may seem harsh but Uncle Joseph has caused one too many problems for my family.

He is a chronic gossiper and interferer. He relishes any opportunity to call my dad and report on the activities of Shereen, Bilal and me.

When it comes to Shereen he is relentless. Her political activism is "disgraceful". "The way she carries on, she'll never find a husband," he says mournfully. "You've allowed her too much freedom, coming and going when she pleases, attending rallies and protests. What man is going to be interested in a girl who parades herself on television with flags and signs, screaming and carrying on?"

My dad doesn't say much in Shereen's defence. He just nods quietly and that is perhaps the most infuriating and hurtful part of it.

So when I see Uncle Joseph at McDonald's I know Dad's mobile phone is going to be active tonight.

"Come over and say hello!" Uncle Joseph cries, leaning over the counter as I attempt to hide myself behind one of the machines.

Emma, the girl serving Uncle Joseph, looks over and rolls her eyes sympathetically at me. I smile at her and come out and shake Uncle Joseph's hand. He moves over to the side of the counter to allow Emma to serve the people behind him.

"So you work here now?" he asks, his eyes greedily taking in every incriminating detail.

I take a deep breath and prepare to be on my best behaviour. I don't want to give him any reason to run back to my father. "Yes, Uncle Joseph," I reply in a sickly-sweet voice. "Twice a week."

"*Night* shift?"

"Well, it's an after-school shift."

He coughs and crosses his arms over his chest. "I'm

surprised your dad allowed you. It's not right that a girl your age works at night. You don't need extra money. You're still at school. Why do you need it? Most young people work to buy these silly DVDs . . . or cigarettes. . ." He looks at me slyly. "Do you smoke?"

"No, of course not!"

He looks at me suspiciously. "I hope not."

"Um, how are Alexandria and Rita?"

He smiles smugly. "My daughters are wonderful. They're such good girls. They're getting excellent grades at university; they're volunteering in the church youth group."

I resist the temptation to tell him that they're both going out with guys years older than them and that their photos are at the entrance to Imperial nightclub.

"I should get going now," he says. "Really, though, your father is mistaken to let you work at such a young age. It's not respectable. Oh well, some people have different standards of parenting to others."

He smiles insincerely at me, grabs his bag of food and walks out. My heart is pounding angrily in my chest. Maybe it's a good thing he left abruptly like that. I might have exploded and made a fool of myself in front of everybody here.

I'm willing to bet my life that he'll be dialling Dad's number before he turns on the car ignition.

"So you saw Uncle Joseph tonight?" my dad asks when he picks me up after work.

I just knew it. Dad must be on Uncle Joseph's speed dial.

"Yeah, I did. I can't stand him!"

He tut-tuts and shakes his head. "Don't be disrespectful, Jamilah."

"Respect should be earned. It shouldn't automatically be given just because somebody happens to have an older birth certificate than me."

He ignores my comment and sighs, concentrating on the road. After a moment's pause he says: "I had my reservations about you working. I knew people would talk. Joseph would never allow his daughters to work at night. Maybe you are too young to be working a night shift."

I turn in a panic towards him. "No, please Dad! Don't take this away from me. Just ignore him. He's going to talk no matter what I do. I'm begging you!"

We're sitting at a traffic light and he looks over at me. I've completely lost all sense of pride and self-respect and tears start crawling down my face. He passes me a tissue and sighs heavily.

"OK, Jamilah. I'm tired of fighting with you. You win this one."

28

Timothy and I are collating our research results. He leans over to my side of the desk to retrieve his pen which has rolled down. He smells of aftershave, mixed with Flex 2-in-1 shampoo and conditioner.

"So, are you an only child?" I ask.

"No. Why do you ask?"

"Because we've already done music, TV shows and celebrity diets."

"I have an older sister, Jessica. She's the publicity director of a company that sells ergonomic office furniture."

"Sounds fascinating. Do you get along?"

"Yeah, like Bush and Saddam at a pool party."

"What's the problem? She doesn't like your cocky attitude?"

He grins and taps his pen on the desk. "Yeah, precisely. She's like my dad. They're obsessed with navy blue suits, long working hours and big fat pay cheques."

"Some people call that ambition."

"Yeah, at being mediocre. All her opinions are cut and pasted from the editorial sections of newspapers. She won't eat at a restaurant unless it rates a mention in the *Sydney Morning Herald Good Food Guide*. If you could buy designer cotton buds she'd be the first in line."

"I don't know if I'd like an office job. It would depend on what I was doing, I guess."

"I know it wouldn't suit me. And the kind of office job my dad wants for me makes me feel like an ice cube in an ice cube tray. You become a perfectly symmetrical, generic mould and pretty soon nobody can tell the difference between you and the other navy suit on the six o'clock train."

"Ahh, the 'I want to be an individual' testimonial. I did that in Grade Five. I came to school with a bob. Not a good idea with manic curls. I ended up getting pelted with salt and vinegar chips by Owen Thompson during recess. Individuality doesn't pay off."

"Sure it does. Being a lemming, like my dad and his colleagues, isn't an attractive way to live."

I smile. "You know something?"

"I know lots of things."

"Apart from your occasional cockiness and irritating confidence—"

"Is there a positive in this sentence?"

"I like talking to you."

"Oh, wow!" He jumps out of his chair and bows. "Thank you. You have made my day. My year. My life."

"Shut up, you dag," I say, motioning at him to sit down. "It's a compliment. Trust me."

"Because my talking abilities are generally looked upon with disdain?"

I laugh. "You said it. Not me."

He raises his eyebrows at me. "You'll get there soon, I think."

"Where?"

"You'll walk into class. And you'll be yourself. And it will be glorious for you."

"You remind me of someone else I know. He's always lecturing me too. You'd like this guy. He doesn't take crap from anybody. He's —"

He suddenly stands up, sweeping his books into his arms. "I'm sick of this assignment. I need a break. How about we finish up tomorrow?"

He doesn't wait for my answer. He walks off, bumping into Liz on his way out.

"Hey Goldfish! Watch it!"

He gives her a devastating look of pity. "I wouldn't bother waking up in the morning if I was *that* pathetic." Then he storms out.

"What a prick!" Liz cries, taking a seat next to me.

"Why'd you call him Goldfish?"

She snorts. "Everybody does. What's the big deal?"

"It's mean."

Amy walks in and approaches us. "This assignment is a bummer," she says, sighing heavily and plonking herself down into a chair. "Oh, hi Liz. It's been a while. Have you taken a moment out of your schedule to speak to us?"

Liz laughs harshly. "That time of the month?"

"No, Liz. There's a far more obvious explanation for my mood."

Liz raises an eyebrow and turns to me. She grabs my arm and looks into my eyes. "Jamie, you need to hear me out. You're making a big mistake. Peter is obviously interested in you. The only reason he hasn't made a move yet is because, believe it or not, he likes you. *Seriously* likes you. And he doesn't want to stuff it up. He says you're different to other girls. He's going to ask you to the formal. But you're screwing it all up. The way you are with Timothy. He's not on Peter's level. Peter's getting pretty confused about where your interests lie."

"Are you suggesting that Jamie should treat Timothy like shit so Peter stays keen?"

"Was I talking to you?" Liz snaps.

"No. You don't do much of that any more. But that's not the point, is it?"

"Hey, let's not argue," I say. "Anyway, I don't know what Peter's on about. Timothy and I were paired up to do this project together. We're not dating, for God's sake."

"He's a loser, Jamie. And yet you seem to enjoy his company."

"Maybe that's because he's nice."

"And because," Amy says, "unlike *some people*, Jamie isn't a fake. She's real and gutsy!"

I don't deserve that, I feel like crying out.

"You're just jealous."

"Of what? Changing my entire personality to fit in with the cool crowd isn't exactly a priority for me. Or Jamie. We're happy to be ourselves."

Liz jumps out of her chair and casts a furious look at Amy. "You're so full of it," she says and stomps away.

"Oh well," Amy says, folding her arms across her chest. "I don't think she even knows who she is any more."

Little does Amy know that it's been a long time since I've been able to look in the mirror and know my own reflection.

29

Tonight's band practice is awesome. Miss Sajda has brought along some albums newly released in the Middle East. There are some Arabic singers performing songs with Italian and French singers, but the rest are mainly Lebanese and Egyptian pop songs with really funky beats. The music is a combination of classical and modern influences: traditional Arabic instruments such as the *darabuka*, the *oud*, the *ney* (like a flute) and the *riq* (a small tambourine), mixed up with the modern electronic Arabic keyboard and Western techno-dance music.

Miss Sajda closes the classroom door and turns up the volume on the stereo so that the music feels as though it's pulsating through my veins. She grins wildly at us, hypnotized by the power of the music. I forget that she's my teacher, that she sets me homework and annoys me with her *Did You Know?* facts and figures about the Arab world. All I can think about is the tingling feeling in the palms of my hands as I hold the *darabuka*, and how my excitement and exhilaration is reflected in her shining eyes.

On Miss Sajda's cue we start to play. I try to make my way through the rhythm of the song, keeping in tune with the beat of the music. Miss Sajda cheers us on and starts to dance across the room. We all laugh and she grins back at us.

When we've finished I look down and notice that my palms are bright red. I collapse back into my chair and Miss Sajda turns the music off.

"Excellent work, everybody!"

"We're going to knock them dead at the formal!" Samira says.

"Just watch out for a guy called Peter Clarkson. If he heckles you, throw a drum at him."

We all pack our instruments away and say our goodbyes. I'm walking out of the door when Miss Sajda calls me back.

"Can I have a word with you, Jamilah?"

I turn around. "Yeah, sure." I put down my *darabuka* case and hop up on to a table.

"Your dad would be proud if he heard you tonight."

I shrug. "So what?"

"What do you mean?"

"I get nothing in return. He won't let me go to my formal.

I'm not particularly interested in his opinion at the moment, given that he doesn't care two bits about mine."

"But he told me you're allowed to play in the band."

"Yes, but I'm not allowed to stay back for my formal."

"Why not?"

"Because it's coed. I'll be the only one in class not allowed to go. Do you have any idea what that kind of humiliation means?"

She leans back in her chair and looks at me thoughtfully. "Well, I'm sure your classmates will understand."

"Understand what?" I cry. "That my father doesn't trust me?"

Her eyes widen in shock. "Of course he trusts you, Jamilah. He's always talking about how proud he is of you and how reliable you are and how pleased he is that you're so well liked at school."

"You know something? You tell me that and I think: big deal. Anyway, I'm *well liked* at school because nobody has a clue about . . . anything. . ."

"What do you mean?"

"Nothing," I say quietly.

She clears her throat and leans towards me. "Don't bottle it all up, Jamilah."

I look at her intently. And I break. "This year has been one big mess! Nobody at school knows about my background. But with me playing in the band it will no longer be a secret. I'm going to look like an idiot! Then there are these guys I'm talking to. Peter's the most popular guy at school and he's interested in me. But he doesn't have a clue that I'm Lebanese-Muslim. Then there's Timothy, who I'm doing a school project with. He's so unbelievably confident and sure of himself! And then there's John, my email buddy. He's the only guy I've ever completely opened up to and it was the most fantastically liberating feeling! But I must have offended him or something because he's blocked my address so that I can no longer send him emails. And my friend, Amy, is going through some sort of personal crisis but refuses to talk to me. It's all falling apart and I have nobody to talk to because talking means I expose myself. And I've been pretending for so long that I can't reverse it all without losing everybody!"

I sink into my chair like a deflating balloon.

She cups my chin in her hand and looks into my eyes. "If they don't know the real you, then you've already lost them, Jamilah."

30

Amy isn't at school today and I text her to see if she's genuinely sick or has just opted for vegetating on the couch in front of Foxtel.

She instantly responds. *I'm ok. Are you 3 2night? I was thinking of coming ova.*

My dad has invited a group of his friends over tonight. This means that they will set up camp in the lounge room, playing cards, drinking Arabic coffee and cups of sweetened mint tea. They'll smoke their water-pipes and cigars, tell Arabic jokes and shake the roof tiles with their roars of laughter.

Shereen has a friend over who is helping her paint banners for an upcoming protest against African poverty. The entire scene is just not the kind of introduction Amy needs to my blissful domestic existence. Yet again I am forced to spin a story and respond to her text message as follows:

Would have loved u 2 but going out 2night with the relos. Won't be back until late. Sorry.

Her response?

NP

That's bad. She didn't even make the effort to write out "no problem", opting instead for a two-letter abbreviation.

I wonder if Amy's getting fed up with me. I wonder why she wants to visit me. There are just too many questions and I've let things go too far to find out the answers.

Amy is away from school again. I ask Liz if she's heard from her but she shakes her head. She's not interested. The only thing that gets her attention now is Sam.

Peter and Chris are in the corridor playing catch with a pencil case. As I approach them on my way to my locker my throat chokes up. Being around Peter always makes me feel like I've got a Land Rover stuck in there.

"Hey Jamie," Peter says, planting himself in front of me. "What do you think about a stand-up comedy act at the formal? It would be so much better than this dumb band idea they've come up with."

"You can't dance to stand-up comedy," I joke.

"We'd make pretty good comedians!" Peter says. "They should have asked us to perform."

"The phrase *penal colony* sent you and Chris into a fit of hysterics in class the other day."

"Exactly," Peter chuckles. "We see the humour in everything."

Timothy and Lindsay Parker enter the corridor. Peter notices and I can practically see his eyes gleam with excitement.

"Well look what we have here," Peter cries. "A goldfish and a FOB. Hey Lindsay, did you find the goldfish on your way to Australia in a boat?"

"You're a comedian," Lindsay says sarcastically.

"Actually, we were just discussing comedy. Maybe Goldfish could provide us with some fish jokes."

Timothy shakes his head and looks at Peter with an expression of pity. "Mate, it takes originality to be a comedian and the goldfish joke is wearing a little thin. Why don't you go look up a book on marine life and come back to me with another name. It might actually make you interesting."

"Ooh, you're funny," Peter says.

"Actually, the only joke I can see around here is you."

Timothy and Lindsay keep on walking and I quickly move on to my locker.

Later in the day Timothy bumps into me.

"Can I ask you something?" he says. "What do you see in him?"

"Who?"

"Peter."

"Nothing!" I say defensively.

"I don't know how you can bear to talk to him after what he did to you."

"Oh, and what am I supposed to do? Ignore him?"

"No. You're supposed to march up to him and inform him that he is the perfect definition of a complete tosser."

I let out a laugh. "That only happens in the movies."

"Why do you want him to like you so badly?"

"I don't! But anyway, there's nothing wrong with wanting to be liked. You just stick to yourself."

"I stick to myself because I'm not interested in changing who I am just to fit in."

"Yeah, but everybody has to do that. Nobody's their real self. It's only when you're at home with your family that your true self comes out."

"I prefer to be consistent."

"That's bull. Everybody puts on an act depending on who they're with."

"What are you so afraid of?"

"I'm not afraid," I say indignantly.

"You sound petrified of something."

"Well I'm not. You don't know the first thing about me."

"Do you know yourself?" He grins at me but I'm not impressed.

"Stick to essays on caviar and molluscs, Socrates. I'll see you around."

I walk off quickly. I'm not interested in being thrown

under the microscope by Timothy yet again. I have a hard enough time looking through the lens myself.

Amy's mother answers the phone. Her voice is frazzled and she's in no mood for small talk. She calls Amy to the phone. I hear Amy's muffled voice in the background. Then an indistinguishable response from Amy's mother.

I wait.

And I wait.

Amy's mother finally returns to the phone. "Amy's asleep," she informs me. She's lying. And she knows I'm not a fool. "I'll get her to call you back."

Amy doesn't.

When I see her in class the following day it's all TV gossip and homework debriefing. A dot-to-dot conversation that leaves no imprint in either of our minds.

31

I practise playing the *darabuka* at home after school. I close my bedroom door, dim the lights and sit on my desk chair. I start to play, my beats getting stronger and deeper as I picture myself onstage at the formal, my true identity exposed. I imagine Peter, Sam, Chris and the rest of their cronies in the audience, jeering at me. I imagine Ahmed, Danielle and Paul looking at me with disgust as it dawns on them that I've sat idly by and allowed Peter to insult and offend. I imagine the look of disappointment on Amy's face. And then I switch scenes. I'm walking on to the stage. I'm standing tall and proud. I'm playing with the band and everybody is cheering.

Cheering for Jamilah.

As I play, and the music takes over me, I realize that I can't deny that I love my Lebanese culture. I love the food. I love the fact that we have such a huge circle of family friends. I love my dad's stories about growing up in Beirut. I love Lebanese weddings and I love Arabic music, especially dancing to the latest pop songs. I love the way our friends stuck by us when my mother died.

All the aunts and uncles fussed over us, and in the first days after my mother had gone they made sure we didn't have a moment to ourselves to sit alone and realize we'd had the hearts and guts wrenched out of our bodies. It was as though her dying was going to send us into starvation mode, because the women brought pots full of food and, in typical Lebanese style, big industrial bags of white rice and lentils and boxes upon boxes of drinks. Our hallway was lined with food and drink supplies from the front door to the kitchen. My dad said that it's a very old cultural tradition to offer condolences and ensure that the house won't be burdened with cooking for people who visit to pay their respects.

All I want is to fit in and be accepted as an Aussie. But I don't know how to do that when I'm juggling my Lebanese and Muslim background at the same time. It's not like juggling an orange, an apple and a banana. They're all fruit and all fruits are pretty much equal, right? But the way I see it, juggling Aussie and Lebanese and Muslim is like juggling a couch, a letter box and a tray of muffins. Completely and utterly incongruous. How can I be three identities in one? It doesn't work. They're always at war with one another. If I want to go clubbing, the Muslim in me says it's wrong and the Lebanese in me panics about bumping into somebody who knows somebody who knows my dad. If I want to go to a Lebanese wedding as the four hundredth guest, the Aussie in me will laugh and wonder why we're not having civilized cocktails in a function room that seats a maximum of fifty people. If I want to fast during Ramadan, the Aussie in me will think I'm a masochist.

I can't win.

32

It's the end of April and the autumn weather has transformed our front lawn into a canvas of orange and brown leaves, fallen acorns and bare trees. I arrive home from school hungry and cold. I walk up our concrete driveway and on to our concrete front porch. On the porch are four green plastic chairs stacked on top of each other. Beside the chairs is an upside-down orange crate that acts as a coffee table. On top of it rests a small steel tray filled with coal, used by my dad when he smokes his water-pipe.

When I open the front door my face is immediately flooded with the warmth of a house alive with the spicy smells of a home-cooked feast. I step into the kitchen and find Aunt Sowsan at the bench, rolling pastries and filling them with spinach and cheese. I can smell lamb and potato roasting in the oven and *mujadara*, brown rice and lentils, cooking on the stove. My stomach starts rumbling and I rush over and hug Aunt Sowsan in excitement.

"Yum! I'm starving," I exclaim.

"Good, that's what I want to hear. Now go inside, change, wash up and come and set the table."

"Where is everybody?"

"Shereen is at uni but will be home soon. Bilal is at work and I've sent your dad and Amo Ameen to the supermarket to get yoghurt and coriander."

I go to my room and return in five minutes, comfortable in jeans and a jumper.

"Aunt Sowsan," I say as I'm setting the table, "if you needed to persuade Dad about something and he was being really stubborn and you couldn't accept no for an answer and you'd run out of plans, what would you do?"

She looks up at me and raises her doughy hands in the air. "Just give me a straight question and I will give you a straight answer, Jamilah."

"Dad won't let me go to my Year Ten formal and it's the end of my life. What do I do?"

She doesn't patronize me with a laugh but seems to be deep in thought as she rolls the last of the pastries and starts laying them out on to the tray.

"What's the objection?"

"It's coed."

"Oh, pretty much case closed."

"Yeah, that's the problem," I say, rolling my eyes. "I bet you if Mum was here things would be different. She would have talked him into it."

Aunt Sowsan laughs. "Is that what you think? Your mother, *Allahyirhamha*" – God rest her soul, – "was the loveliest, kindest women I've ever known. She snuggled her way into my heart. She was also one of the toughest, strictest mothers. Shereen and Bilal went through what you're going through but it was your mother who was head of discipline in the house – not your father."

"*What?*"

"That's right. Your father was the easy one."

"*Easy?* If the reproductive cycle of tigers is being shown on the Discovery channel he changes the channel because he thinks it's not nice for me to watch!"

She bursts out laughing.

I lean across the kitchen bench and pick a cucumber out of the salad. "Are you telling me that Mum, *Allahyirhamha*, was stricter than Dad? My dad? Your brother? Did you somehow fail to notice the charter of curfew rights stuck on the fridge?"

"I did notice it, yes." She gives me a cheeky smile. "Very nicely typed."

"You're doing the sibling loyalty thing on me!" I say with a pout.

"Do you want to know about your mother or not?"

I reach out for another piece of cucumber, crunch down into it and nod.

"OK, well I remember when Shereen turned fifteen and her best friend, Hala, was having her birthday party on a cruise boat around the harbour. It was your mother who said no because she'd heard that Hala's uncles and aunts would be drinking and she refused to have Shereen in any environment where there was alcohol."

"What did Dad say?"

"He thought it was OK because it was the adults who were drinking and they'd be supervising. Your mother insisted that Shereen could not go."

I don't say anything and keep munching on the cucumber.

"When Shereen was your age she wanted a second earring. Your father gave her permission but your mother said that she was too young. If your mother was home, Bilal and Shereen knew that they couldn't watch *Neighbours* or *Home and Away*. If Shereen brought home any magazines, like *Cleo* or *Cosmopolitan*, they went straight into the rubbish bin. Your mother insisted that Bilal help with the chores. There was none of this, 'he's a boy' business with her. If Shereen or Bilal wanted anything, they'd run to your dad first because he was the softie."

My mouth is wide open and I take a seat on the kitchen stool to stop myself from doing a horizontal on the floor.

"You might want to swallow the cucumber before you look at me in shock," Aunt Sowsan says with a chuckle.

I shut my mouth but it takes me a few seconds to swallow the cucumber which has to bypass a huge lump of confusion lodged in my throat. I finally summon the sense to put some words together and say: "So then why . . . I mean, how come . . . I mean, with me. . ."

I still don't seem to be able to construct a sentence and Aunt Sowsan gives me a gentle smile. "People change, Jamilah. When your mother passed away your father's role suddenly changed. When your mother was alive your father's primary job was to drive the taxi and support the family. He worked long shifts – longer than he does now. The house was your mother's domain. She cooked, she cleaned, she ironed, she washed, she made sure you all did your homework, she went to parent-teacher interviews, she checked report cards, she threw all her energy and purpose into raising you. Your father threw all his energy and purpose into supporting you. With your mother's death, the roles merged. Don't you think he was scared?"

"*Scared*? Of what?"

"Of failing, Jamilah. Of being a single parent. Of how people would judge him. He has had to raise three children. Don't you think he worries about the fact that you don't have a mother to be there for you through your teenage years? Or that Shereen is a young lady now and will perhaps soon fall in love but not know who to talk to or ask for guidance? Or that with your father's hours behind the taxi wheel he hasn't had the chance to stay on Bilal's back and keep him motivated and focused enough to finish school?"

"Yeah, but why am I being punished for his fears? How does Dad being so strict with me make it any easier for me at school? With my friends?"

"You've had to grow up faster than others, Jamilah. That's what death does to a person. It rips away the innocence and naivety and throws you out to the world. Most people have the luxury of never having to try to understand their parents until they're grown up – sometimes it takes *being* a parent to understand your own parents. But when one half of your life is suddenly torn away from you, you owe it to the other half to speed up that process. To try and understand what your father is going through. That's part of the healing death forces upon people." She takes a deep sigh and looks up above. "May Allah protect us from any further tragedy and rest your mother's soul. Ameen."

33

Mustafa plants his chair in front of my desk, throws a pad of paper and a pen in front of me, and proceeds to stare intently at my face.

"Something wrong?" I ask.

"What rhymes with incinerator, man?"

"Huh?"

"What rhymes with incinerator?"

"Um . . . terminator?"

He slaps his hand to his forehead. "Of course!" He leans over my desk and scribbles *terminator* down on the paper, writing some notes beside it, his tongue protruding slightly as he focuses on the task.

I giggle and he looks up in surprise. "What's so funny?"

"Nothing."

"You dig Snoop Dog?"

"He's OK."

"Just OK?"

"Yeah." I shrug my shoulders.

"You need mental rehabilitation. What about Nelly?"

"He's cool. The band-aid on his cheek is a bit dumb though."

"Do you reckon he ever wears Disney band-aids?"

I'm about to laugh when I note the serious look on his face.

"Um, I'm not sure."

"Because that would be cool. If he did go with the whole cartoon theme, though, he should go with Looney Tunes. Not Bugs Bunny because he's a bit too up himself. I reckon Road Runner or Tasmanian Tiger. They're bad but cool, you know? It fits with his image. It's all about your image, man."

"Mmm . . . right, Mustafa."

He shifts in his chair, sits upright and starts tapping the pen against the table. "So why are you so worried about playing at your formal?"

I sigh. "It's complicated."

He cocks his head to one side. "The best things that happen to us are always complicated. Man, you have to get your hands dirty to have fun."

I roll my eyes at him. "Mustafa, quit the counselling effort."

"Hey, last year your hair was darker."

I give him a look that clearly indicates that I think he's crazy.

"Just an observation. . ."

"Yeah, well, I distinctly recall you had a mullet, and there was a lot more hair connecting your eyebrows then too."

He looks at me sheepishly and then suddenly breaks out into a wide grin. "That's a good one! I might use that in 'Dig Me For Who I Am Not Whatchya See'."

"I take it that's on your album?"

"Yeah, but it needs a bit of work. I'm busy writing a new song. It's about my friends, Enrico and Wayne and Omar. How the cops keep giving them a hard time, on their backs you know, every time they're out at the shops, just hanging out . . . all innocent and stuff. That song's going to be deep! About ethnic pride and the bloody cops and their racism."

"Wayne's not an ethnic name."

"Yeah OK, so he's as Anglo as you can get. But he sympathizes."

I look at him cynically.

"OK, OK. So I'll make the song about cops and how they stick it to us guys in the hood."

"What hood would that be? New York?"

"Do you see an Eiffel Tower around here?"

I repress an outburst of laughter. "It's called the Statue of Liberty."

He waves his hand as if to brush my correction off as irrelevant. "Same thing. Anyway, it's the Sydney hood. The Westie hood."

"Yeah . . . right."

He gives me an exasperated look and leans back in his chair, studying me like I'm a biology assignment.

"What's going on, Jam?" he says softly.

"Nothing."

"You ashamed of something?"

"No!"

He leans his face in close to mine. "I'm sorry we were a bit rough with you about your decision. We were so moved by the injustice that we felt inspired to rap about your plight. Want to hear?"

"Um, yeah, sure."

He clears his throat and kicks off:

"They say it's about tradition
But it's really about inhibition
They say it's about protection
But they're denying us the right to make our own election
The parents need to chill
And stop interfering with our free will."

Mustafa finishes, looking down at me with a triumphant expression on his face.

"That was . . . really deep. Thanks."

He grins proudly at me. After a few moments he says: "Can I just say this to you, homey girl? I know you don't want to play because you're embarrassed. You have nothing to be ashamed of. If you dig what you're doing, they'll love you too. Do you think I walk around worrying whether people will dig my rap music? I'm an artist. I respect my art. People

200

can see that and they respect me for it. Man, we've got a rich identity! We've got our feet dipped in different cultures. It's cool! Embrace it!"

He smiles, stands up and returns his chair to his desk. For the rest of the class I observe him poring over his pad of paper, writing and crossing things out, tapping his feet to some imaginary beat, his forehead furrowed in concentration.

I've never really taken Mustafa seriously. He thinks the Eiffel Tower is a New York landmark. He believes that a band-aid on his cheek makes him look tough.

And yet, he seems a lot less confused than me.

34

Aunt Sowsan has invited my family and Miss Sajda to her place for a Sunday barbecue. In typical style, there is enough meat, chicken and bread to feed a country town, and we're all gathered around the outdoor table in the backyard demolishing it all. Aunt Sowsan has made side dishes of pasta salad, potato salad, a creamy garlic dip, humous and tabouli.

My dad insists I sit at the table with the adults and not hide myself with my plate in front of the television.

"Make sure you eat garlic," my dad warns me and laughs. "Otherwise you'll smell it on everybody else's breath."

I grab a piece of bread, fold a piece of chicken into it and dress it with a teaspoon of the garlic dip.

"Advice taken!" I cry and gulp it down.

"Did you hear that, Sowsan?" my dad cries. "Jamilah took my advice. God be praised!"

We all laugh and continue devouring the feast. Not that our efforts have made any impression on the plates. You know that you're at Aunt Sowsan's house if everybody has managed to stuff their faces three times over but the plates of food look no different to when you started.

It is perhaps the one issue on which Shereen and Aunt Sowsan argue. Shereen gets pretty upset about the fact that so much food goes to waste when there are people starving in the world. She's quite right, but it's a habit entrenched in Arabic culture and Aunt Sowsan would consider herself to be dishonouring her guests if she didn't make such an exorbitant amount.

It always feels odd to be sitting at the same table as Miss Sajda, eating and socializing outside of madrasa hours. But she fits in well and even Amo Ameen, who's usually so quiet, is inspired to joviality and is cracking jokes and making everybody roar with laughter. I don't particularly find the Arabic jokes funny, but that's because I don't understand the punchlines or the context. I just pretend to laugh on their cue. That's purely a protective measure designed to avoid my dad feeling sympathy for me and translating the jokes into English. Hearing him inject Aussie slang into an Arabic joke doesn't make for very comic material.

Miss Sajda and my dad are doubled over with laughter as Amo Ameen launches into a new joke. I get up to help Aunt

Sowsan and Shereen clear the food away and start on the dishes. Miss Sajda jumps up to help.

"No, stay," Aunt Sowsan insists, motioning for Miss Sajda to sit down.

"No, I'll help," Miss Sajda says, starting to pick up plates.

"I won't hear of it," Aunt Sowsan says. "Sit down and enjoy my husband's good mood while it lasts!"

Amo Ameen grins and Miss Sajda shrugs and takes her seat again. "If you insist."

"I do," Aunt Sowsan says, much to my disappointment. We need as many hands as we can get. The downfall of Aunt Sowsan's mammoth meals is the amount of washing-up afterwards. It takes half an hour to eat and half the day to clean up.

I'm grumbling about the washing load to Shereen as we walk to the kitchen with a pile of plates in each of our hands.

"Tell me about it," she mutters. "Dad and Amo Ameen could get off their butts and at least bring their plates to the sink. God, male sexism kills me."

"I know!"

"What are you two whispering about?" Aunt Sowsan asks, poking her head between our shoulders as we enter the kitchen.

"The fact that this world is chauvinistic," Shereen says. "Women cook and clean and men get fat on the food and get a cup of tea after dinner as well. It drives me bonkers."

"I agree," I say.

Shereen looks at me in surprise. "We have a Guinness Book of Records moment here!"

I stick my tongue out at her. "Don't worry, I'm not fully converted. I still think hairspray shouldn't be banned."

"Environmental hazard."

"So are my curls."

"Well, my generation is generally different," Aunt Sowsan says. "But men are improving."

"Excuse me?" Shereen scoffs. "What about our beloved brother, Bilal?"

Aunt Sowsan pauses. "Ah, yes. Bilal – a mystery."

After an hour in the kitchen, with our hands wrinkly from the warm water and our backs sore from standing over the sink, we're finally able to sit down again with cups of tea and pieces of cake and Arabic sweets. We devour the pastries filled with dates and the biscuits coated with chocolate and layered with strawberry jam.

Whilst Aunt Sowsan and Shereen are inside praying the afternoon prayer, Amo Ameen asks me a question and inadvertently opens a big, fat, juicy can of worms.

"So you're in Year Ten now, Jamilah?" he asks. It's not often that Amo Ameen addresses me, but he's uncharacteristically chatty today so I go with the flow.

"That's right," I reply.

"Don't you have a special function in Year Ten? Like a dance or something? I remember Shereen going when she was your age."

I look over at my dad and his face tenses.

"Yes we do," I say. "The formal. But Dad won't let me go." I jut my chin out defiantly, waiting for my dad to respond.

"Why not, Hakim?" Amo Ameen asks innocently.

My dad puffs on his water-pipe and looks at Amo Ameen. "I have my reasons, Ameen."

"Yeah, but they're not valid!" I cry.

My dad puts down his pipe and sighs. "Do we have to go through this again, Jamilah?"

"I just don't get it. What's the big deal? I'm not going with a guy. I'll go with my girlfriends."

This is rather a difficult prospect but if I can only get permission, I'll do whatever it takes to drag one of the girls from my class with me.

"When will you ever trust me?" I ask.

Miss Sajda and Amo Ameen squirm uncomfortably in their seats as they watch my father and I do battle.

"How many times must I explain to you that I do trust *you*? It's the people around you that I don't trust. And then there's your reputation. What will our friends say if they know you were out late at a party where there is drinking and dancing and God knows what else."

"Who cares what people think? I'm so sick and tired of caring what the oldies in our community think. All they do is gossip. It doesn't matter what you do, they'll find an excuse to talk."

"We don't need to make it easy for them."

"It's not like you defend us anyway!" I yell. "You let them talk and talk and you don't ever come to our defence! Uncle

206

Joseph lectures you about us being disgraces and *too free* and you sit back and take it!"

My father recoils, as though I've slapped him in the face. I can't bear to look at him and I jump out of my chair and rush in the house, locking myself in the bathroom.

35

The Polaroid is in an old bottle-green album, wedged in between a photograph of my sister and me striking a pose for the camera, and a picture of Bilal giving me a piggyback ride. Next to it, in my mother's handwriting, is a small note: *Baladna algadeed*. Our New Country.

My father stands with his arms looped lazily around my mother's shoulders. They're in the international terminal at Sydney airport. My father's grin is framed by a thick black moustache. His hair is high and thick, like a ball of steel wool. My mother's smile manages to convey both fear and excitement. She's dressed in flared green pants, puffy white shirt and has gigantic copper sunglasses perched on her head. Her red henna hair is slicked back into a ponytail.

The photo has always tugged at me. Pulled me to it when I've missed her and when I've worried that I've forgotten the shape of her eyes and the contour of her cheekbones.

"What are you doing?" my father asks. I can tell that he's trying to sound indifferent. There's still a bit of tension between us since our fight the other day.

"Just looking at photos."

He clears his throat. "Of who?"

"You and Mum."

He approaches me slowly, peering over my shoulder at the open page of the album.

He lets out a chuckle and then abruptly tries to stop it. "I haven't seen that photo in ages."

"Mum was gorgeous. You know, you could have done with some hair gel."

He sits next to me on the couch and smiles. "It was our first plane ride. We arrived in Sydney hungry. We thought we had to pay for the aeroplane meals. So we hardly ate and kept refusing every time they brought a tray around."

"Are you kidding?"

"Your mother and I were startled at how easily everybody else accepted each meal." He chuckles and shakes his head. "We had few savings as it was and weren't going to spend them all on food."

"Why didn't you ask somebody?"

He snorts. "Pride. We arrived in Sydney with two

suitcases, a Lebanese flag, one photo album and a prayer mat. I was not going to advertise the fact that we had so little by demanding to know the price of food."

"You know something, Dad, you were a major dag." I smile cheekily at him as I touch the photo. "You seriously needed to apply some hair product to that afro."

"It was the fashion then. I'm sure Bilal's children will tease him about his porcupine spikes and your children will ask you why you dyed your hair yellow."

I slowly turn the pages of the album. And then suddenly he stops me. He tenderly touches a photograph of my mother sitting on the bonnet of a bottle-green Datsun 12Y. She's grinning wildly at the camera.

My father slaps his hands down on his thighs and bursts out laughing.

"Ya Allah! I remember that day! That was the first last time I took your mother out for a driving lesson. She managed to drive without incident all along Parramatta Road but then reversed into a parked car *on our street*!" He continues to laugh. "I was furious. You know why?"

I shrug.

"She wouldn't stop laughing. She just wrecked the rear of my brand-new Datsun and she was in hysterics!"

I can't help but laugh along with him.

"I was getting so worked up, losing my temper and pacing up and down the street and she was doubled over in laughter. Pretty soon she had me laughing too. That's how she was. She'd kill me if I messed up the linen closet or dropped a pan but she had a way of calming me down. I loved her contradictions.

"She was a wise and wonderful woman, Jamilah. We always complimented our friends. *You're so wise, so funny, so smart.* We always laughed at our friends' jokes and were cheerful when we saw them. Were always switched on for our friends. We wanted them to go away and tell others: *That Hakim, he is a nice man. Always laughing and happy and hospitable.* But to those closest to us, we felt we did not have to pretend. We felt we had the right to come home in a bad mood and not talk if we didn't feel like it without caring how the other person felt."

It's the first time my dad has ever been so candid with me about his relationship with my mother. I stare up at him, soaking it in.

"She was the closest person to me on earth and I never told her I admired her strength of conviction and her sharp wit and her kind heart. I wish I had spent every day with her as though it were our last."

"Were you happy?"

"Yes, we were very happy. We could laugh and talk; we could sit comfortable in silence. Our moods matched like pieces in a jigsaw puzzle. Of course, the pieces didn't always fit, as with all marriages. Since your mother's death I've fallen in love with her many times over. . . *Khalas.* Enough. What is done is done. I am fifty-two years old and I have three children to raise. It is just that sometimes, Jamilah, I wonder how I am to do this alone. . ."

His voice fades away as he takes the album from me and fingers the edges of the photographs. "I've never asked you this before," he says, his voice solemn and guarded. "Have you ever thought . . . I mean, have you ever considered that I might remarry one day?"

His question takes me by surprise. It's not that it hasn't occurred to me before. When I see my dad sitting up late at night, smoking his cigarettes, drinking his coffee and staring at the floor, I think it might be nice for him. To have someone to hold at night. To have someone to watch *M.A.S.H* reruns and Egyptian sitcoms with over cups of tea and salted mixed nuts.

"It's OK," he says, interpreting my silence. "You don't have to answer me."

I'm glad. Because I don't want to tell him that the selfish part of me wants him to be alone. Alone with only the memory of my mother to comfort him on those nights he sits and stares.

36

Tonight I'm on my break at work when Timothy comes by on his bike. I see him and my insides go all funny, like they do the moment before you're about to board an upside-down roller-coaster.

"Don't tell me – undercooked chops again?" I ask.

"No, this time it was undercooked fish fingers." He leans his bike against the table and takes a seat across from me. "You know what that means, don't you?"

"They go all soggy and the bread gets moist and the whole thing becomes a disaster?"

"Precisely. I love my nan, but since we moved in with her I haven't had a decent meal. My mum works late nights and doesn't really have time to cook. I'm one of those toast-burning guys so I'm usually on a diet of fast food."

"Do you mind me asking you why your mum chose to move to Guildford?"

He hesitates for a moment and then shrugs. "When my mum left my dad she decided to live with my nan and look after her more. It was kind of her way of making up for lost time. She neglected my nan all the years she was with my dad."

"Is it as hard as they say?"

"What?"

"Divorce. I know what it feels like to be raised by one parent. But I think it'd be so awkward living between two houses, getting stuck in the middle, dividing your loyalties."

"I don't have a problem with that. My loyalty's firmly with my mum. My dad was cheating on my mum for years. My mum knew that but she stayed for the sake of me and Jessica. That drives me mental, but let's not go there."

"So what made her finally decide to leave?"

"It's funny but it was something very stupid and simple. She found my dad's girlfriend's eyebrow tweezer in the car and it set her off. She went ballistic. All this pent-up anger exploded and she packed her bags then and there and left to go stay with my nan. I followed her a couple of days later."

"It's funny how small things can set people off. I

remember the time my dad. . ." I quickly cut myself off.

"You remember the time. . .?"

I smile shyly. "Never mind. It's not important."

"Do you usually expect people to open up to you in exchange for nothing?"

"I'm not used to talking about my dad. . ."

"So start."

I pause and look at him closely. I see trust and honesty and loyalty in his smile. "I was just going to say that after my mother died my dad kind of fell apart. Have you ever been around silence? The kind of silence that weighs a house down? Like thick, murky, humid air, it sucks the noise and sound out of a place. My dad barely spoke to us. And then one day he was cleaning out our laundry and he found an old hairclip that belonged to my mum. It had fallen behind the washing machine. He just stood there, bawling. I have no idea what went on in his mind but he started looking into our eyes again after that. He reclaimed his voice and he hasn't stopped talking since."

"My mum did the opposite. She was suddenly alone and desperate to convince herself it was fine. She threw herself into a Masters degree, voluntary work, painting classes, yoga. It drove me crazy. It was like she was trying to make sure that she was busy for every last minute of the day. That way she'd never have to deal with anything."

"So I take it things are ugly between your parents now?"

"Whenever I have weekend visits with my dad he complains about my *irresponsible* mother hauling me over to the *slums of Sydney* to live with her *senile mother*. He has never stepped foot over this side of the city. I honestly reckon he thinks he needs to be immunized or to apply for a visa to get over the Bridge."

"Do you ever miss him?"

"The bimbo hanging off his arm makes it hard to feel any sense of loss. I know lots of people in class wonder about me: where I've come from, why I'm here and not in some prestigious school on the North Shore. But I couldn't care less."

"Really?" I say, grinning. "I hadn't noticed."

"This is weird," he says after a moment's thought.

"What is?"

He squirms uncomfortably in his seat. "I don't usually do this."

"Do what?"

"I don't do personal. I don't talk about family stuff. With anybody."

I smile. "Me neither."

Uncle Joseph somehow sees me talking to Timothy. My dad now thinks I have a boyfriend and that I only wanted a job so that I could organize secret meetings with him.

"He goes to school with me and *no* I didn't ask him to meet me at work. He happens to live close by and, would you believe it, he felt like a Big Mac!"

"Do not talk to me in that tone of voice, Jamilah! Uncle Joseph said that you were in a very compromising situation. How many times have I told you to be careful about your reputation?"

"Dad!" I cry, jumping from my chair in frustration. "Whose word do you trust? Mine or Uncle Joseph's? There is nothing going on between me and Timothy. It was an innocent conversation."

"But people—"

"How about I lock myself up in my bedroom for the rest of my life? That way we never have to worry about what people will say."

My dad raises his voice. "Do not mock me, Jamilah!"

"I obey your will. I follow your curfew rules. You don't appreciate me! I might as well go behind your back because you think I do anyway."

And so that's what I decide to do. I'm fed up with the rules and fights. I'm angry with my dad and I want to get back at him. So when Liz invites me to go to the movies after school with her, Sam and Peter, I don't fumble for an excuse to get out of the invitation. I say yes.

I call Bilal. He's at the gym and unimpressed with my call as I have interrupted his bicep curl repetition session. I beg him to delay his plans for tonight and pick me up. He reluctantly agrees, warning me that I'll be pet food if Dad finds out what we're doing.

Then I call my dad.

"I need to go to Amy's house tonight."

"Why?"

"We have an overnight test. We have to hand it in tomorrow and our teacher has made us work in pairs."

"She's welcome to come to our place."

He is so predictable. I have an answer ready. "Her mum needs her to be home tonight. She's not feeling well and needs someone around."

There's a long pause.

"Dad?"

"I have a late shift tonight. Who will pick you up?"

"I checked with Bilal. He said he can."

"So you asked him before you asked me?"

"*Dad*," I moan. "I just wanted to cover all my bases before I bothered you." I bite down hard on my lip, praying that he'll take the bait.

"I want you home by nine. And this is not to become a habit."

"OK, sure," I say jokingly, "I'll tell the Board of Education to review the way they assign their tests so it aligns with your rules."

"Yes, you do that," he responds. I can sense that he's trying to hold back a laugh and I suddenly feel guilty about lying to him.

And yet the temptation is so strong. It's like being on a diet and being confronted with a slice of mud cake. You decide to devour it and deal with the consequences the next day: an extra-long run on the treadmill, a compensatory day of carrots and celery. I don't think my dad would appreciate the analogy but that's the way I rationalize it as I hop on to the bus with Liz, Sam and Peter.

I wonder what Amy would think. She's absent from school again so I don't have to face her today. Somehow I don't think she'd approve.

As soon as we arrive at the cinema complex Liz and Sam decide that they're "famished". They give Peter and I pathetic, wide-eyed looks of despair and rub their tummies.

"I *must* eat food," Sam says.

"OK, grab a burger meal and take it into the cinema with you." My voice is desperate. We have fifteen minutes until the next movie session begins. If we miss it, the next session doesn't start for another hour. That means I won't get home by nine.

"I hate eating a burger over my lap," Liz complains, pouting at me. "It's so icky and messy. And I like to eat one chip and then take a bite of the burger. There's a system involved."

"How *cute*," Sam says, grabbing her from her waist and whacking a big sloppy kiss on her neck.

I start to panic. If I insist on the earlier session I'll be the whingeing odd one out. But if I don't, I'll get home late and my dad is likely to send out an Australian Federal Police task force with sniffer dogs to look for me.

"I hate to be the party pooper," I say meekly, "but do you mind if we see this session? It's just that my brother's picking me up and he can't come by later."

"You can hitch a ride with me," Peter offers. "My brother's picking me up too cos he's free tonight."

My heart starts racing like an Olympic athlete sighting the finish line. So I keep spinning a web of lies. "Thanks but we're going out afterwards so he has to pick me up anyway."

"Well I'm hungry!" Liz says, looking at me with an annoyed expression on her face. "I wish you'd told me that when I invited you."

I want to thump her on the head with a blunt instrument. Has she always been so selfish?

We end up deciding to see a different movie. One that allows Liz to eat her meal according to her wretched system and me to get picked up on time. We grab some food and because Peter, Sam and Liz all want to smoke we take our food outside and hang out on a bench in the car park.

"Want a drag?" Peter asks. We're sitting up on the bench, our feet resting on the seat. We're so close that our legs are touching. He blows the smoke close to my face and I can't help but cough. He bursts out laughing.

"You dag! You can't go coughing every time somebody blows smoke in your face. It's not cool. Here, I'll teach you how to take a drag."

My eyes dart maniacally to the left and right, searching for any familiar faces passing by in the car park. There's every possibility that somebody we know might see me. But I ignore my conscience and put the cigarette to my lips. I cough and splutter and Peter points at me and laughs with Sam and Liz. I feel like an idiot.

"You just need practice," he says. He takes the cigarette from me and inhales. "You know, you're pretty innocent, Jamie. But you don't fool me. I reckon you've got lots of dark secrets."

"What makes you say that?" I stammer.

He taps his temple with his finger. "Trust me, I know these things. I think there's a wild side to you. Like they say, you've gotta watch out for the quiet ones."

"Well, what you see is what you get," I say in an unconvincing voice. "So are you excited about the formal?" I smile broadly, trying to steer the conversation in another direction.

"Yeah, but I'm still pissed off about the band. You can't dance to Middle Eastern music."

"You need props," Sam says. "Like camels or bombs." They let out a big hoot of laughter.

"My dad thinks it's just political correctness," Peter says. "The school's obviously trying to suck up to the minorities."

I clear my throat and play with my fingernails. This is wrong. I regret being here. I want to be around people who make me feel good about myself and who bring out the best in me. But I'm sitting here listening to my heritage being rubbished and I'm a mute.

I can't help but think of Timothy. There's so much courage and fire in him. He can be quiet and unassuming and then bold and daring. He walks around the school knowing that Peter and his entourage spread rumours about him being a snob because he used to live on the North Shore. And yet he holds his head up. He refuses to wear a bullet-proof vest to protect against their words, words that shoot out and pierce the skin. He's like a football player who runs out on to the field without any protection. No mouthguard or knee and elbow padding. He's ready to tackle anyone, but he does it without any fierce need to prove a point.

I want to be like that. I've got so much protective padding strapped to myself that it's suffocating my voice, my conscience, my personality.

And then there's the guilt.

Trust. It's all I've ever wanted from my dad.

I've defended myself. Argued that I'm worthy of it. That my word is my honour. That he can snuggle up to it and sleep well through the night.

But I'm betraying my father and the hypocrisy is sitting in my stomach like an undigested sandwich.

I sit and listen to the three of them ramble on about a world wholly foreign to my own: nightclubs and joints and getting pissed and doing "it" and picking on *losers* like Ahmed and Paul in the locker room.

Then Peter notices two Indian ladies walking up the stairs in their colourful saris. He cups his hands to his mouth and yells out: "*Curry Munchers!*" Liz and Sam cackle and Peter looks thoroughly pleased with himself.

The movie is a blur. All I can see is Amy shaking her head at me. All I can hear are Timothy's words of disappointment. And my father? He's sitting in an armchair, his *argeela* in one hand, a cup of tea in the other, smoking my betrayal, drinking in my deceit.

After the movie, we go to the car park, where Peter's brother is waiting. They decide to hang out at a nearby park.

"Come along," Peter says. "My brother's brought along some beer. We'll play truth or dare. We can find out about your *wild* side." He winks at me and I feel dirty. I turn the offer down, reminding them about my other commitments.

They jump into the car and leave me waiting alone in the dark. I stand under the cinema entrance lights and wait for Bilal.

I take one foot into the car and he raises his hand in the air. "Stop!"

"What's wrong?"

"You *stink* of smoke!"

I pull my hair and clothes to my nose. It's as though I've taken a bath in an ashtray.

"Have you been smoking?"

"I took one drag. It sucks. I have no idea why you do it."

"You can't go home smelling like that. Dad will know as soon as I turn the car into our driveway!"

"He's working late."

"He told me he'll be home by nine." He leans his head on the steering wheel. "What are we going to do?"

I throw my jacket into the back seat. "I'll wash my hair."

"I told you he'll probably be home by the time we arrive."

"Wait here."

I run to the cinema toilets. I pick a basin. I tip my head over into the sink. I glance over at the soap dispenser to my right, take a deep sigh and do what I know I have to.

I start to wash my hair with the soap from a cinema-toilet soap dispenser.

It is as disgusting and moronic as it sounds. I scrub and scrub, and when I'm satisfied that I've worked up a decent enough lather, I reach out to turn the tap on.

Except there's no tap. Just a faucet.

I look up at half an angle, my hair dripping with soapsuds; my eyes squinting through the water and soap that's dribbling down my face. I realize that Hoyts has decided to go high tech on its patrons. The faucet operates with a sensor so I have to position my head at a certain angle to get the water to run. It was already going to be tough work to rinse my hair with my head upside down in a tiny sink. Try adding a stupid sensor to the equation and you have a recipe for disaster.

I'm in a panic now. I'm rinsing as much as I can, frantically twisting my head into different angles every three seconds as the water keeps on stopping.

I eventually throw my head back, crack my neck muscles which have gone into a spasm, and tie my hair into a bun. I look shocking. My eye make-up has run down my face, my hair looks greasy with soap, and the front of my top is drenched. It will have to do. I rush out of the bathroom, ignoring people's stares.

Bilal gives me a pitiful look.

"Was it worth it?" he asks.

"I don't know what is any more," I say, and burst into tears.

37

Dad and Bilal are having a fight. I've never seen them at each other like this. It's past three on Saturday morning when I hear shouting. I've been on tenterhooks ever since the movie, but Dad doesn't seem to suspect anything and this fight doesn't sound as though it's about me. I get out of bed and peek out from my door. Bilal is in the kitchen, leaning against the bench and drinking a glass of water. He has obviously just arrived home. My dad is screaming at him: "How dare you walk into our home at this hour smelling of alcohol and smoke!"

I think Bilal is drunk because he slams the glass of water down on to the bench and yells back: "You drove me to it,

Dad! I come home this afternoon and tell you that my mate's boss thinks I've got a real talent at fixing cars and you frigging have a go at me about getting a real job! And then you wonder why I don't talk to you."

My dad's face suddenly turns shades of purple and red. He looks like he's about to combust. I wonder whether our supply of soap is going to be big enough for this fight.

"Is this how you talk to your father?" he shrieks in Arabic. "Where is your respect? You speak to me like I am some person off the street! I am your father! Do you hear me? You come to my home drunk? With two sisters in the house, you dare to disrespect them?"

Usually Bilal would calm down after being told off like that. He would realize that he's overstepped the mark. But he must have really had too much to drink because he actually sneers at my dad and says: "You don't listen to what I want. Well, it's my life not yours."

My nervous system just about collapses when I see him challenge Dad like that. Shereen then hurricanes out of her bedroom and throws herself in the middle of Dad and Bilal.

"Shut up, Bilal! Go to your room!"

"Stay out of this, Shereen," Bilal yells back.

"I said get inside!" she orders him.

"This is between Bilal and me, Shereen," Dad cries.

"Dad, just calm down. It's the middle of the night. The neighbours are going to call the cops on us with all this yelling. Bilal will go inside and it can be sorted out in the morning."

Dad starts muttering under his breath and Bilal looks at Shereen, shakes his head, and storms out of the room, banging the kitchen door shut on his way out. He passes me in the corridor and gives me a brief look. His eyes are bloodshot and I shrink back in fright. He doesn't address or acknowledge me but goes into his bedroom, slamming the door behind him. I bite down on my quivering lip to stop myself from crying. I stand in the doorway for four or five minutes, scared to even raise an eyelid in case Dad hears and realizes I've been watching. I start to feel pins and needles attack my toes and feet and I finally muster up the courage to turn around and climb back into bed.

It must be two hours later when I wake up. Shereen is snuggled up beside me, clusters of tissues around her pillow. I sink my head into my pillow and hug her close, wondering, not for the first time, if things would have been different if our mother was around.

When I wake up later that morning I find a note from Shereen on the pillow beside me:

Jam, I'll be in the city today, at the rally against the war in Iraq. Tell Dad you guys should go ahead and have dinner without me. I doubt I'll make it back in time. Love you – and try to keep the peace this morning between them.
Tree-hugger xxoo

I try to detect any noises which might indicate that either Dad or Bilal are awake. Soon enough I hear Dad's smoker's cough, the sound of his heavy slippers against the kitchen floorboards and the whistle of the kettle.

I jump out of bed, have a shower and get changed. I tap on Bilal's door but there's no response, only the faint sound of his snores. I breathe a sigh of relief. I'm not in the mood for adopting the role of United Nations peacemaker at breakfast.

"Morning," I say, entering the kitchen and kissing my dad on the forehead.

"Morning," he answers, smiling wearily at me.

He doesn't look like he's had a lot of sleep and it occurs to me that he doesn't have anybody to hug him in bed. That when he goes to bed angry or upset with us, he has nobody to complain to or confide in. That in between the bickering and the working and the paying of the bills and the juggling of three personalities, there must also be loneliness. It hits me so suddenly that for a moment I want to reach out to my dad and hug him. But something holds me back and I know what it is: my lack of courage. I always seem to lack the courage to translate my conscience into action, to go from thinking good to doing good. As I stare at my dad moving quietly about the kitchen preparing his ritual morning cup of coffee, I feel an intense sadness. For the first time I see him for what he is – a lonely man. But there's such a gulf of misunderstanding between us that I don't know how to make up for it.

*

Take away human noises from a house and you're left with a humming refrigerator, the ticking of wall clocks and the creaking sounds of wood expanding in the roof.

Bilal leaves as soon as he wakes up. He wants to "chill out" somewhere in the city.

My father has another madrasa meeting with Miss Sajda and the other staff members. He leaves the house smelling of musk and cigarettes, muttering about Bilal and insolent behaviour.

I walk around the house. I picture Amy in the lounge room, relaxed on the couch with a bag of chips and good conversation. My mother is in the kitchen cooking up a feast, smiling down on us as she soaks crushed wheat and chops up parsley.

I try to picture another woman in her place. But then I push the thought to the part of my brain which deals with such things in the shadows of the night.

Computer time, and the sound of the keyboard competes with music I've downloaded from the net. I send an email to John. Just for kicks. Just to know if he's still a candidate for a missing persons ad.

My email is still blocked.

But wait. I look closely. There is a sign of life.

My hotmail messenger indicates that **Rage_Against_ The_Machine** is online.

I'm about to send a message when my mobile rings.

The call changes everything.

Shereen is on the other end. She's been arrested with

five of her friends and is in custody at a nearby police station.

I lose my grip on the phone and it drops on to the floor. I sweep down to get it, practically dropping it again my hands are shaking so much.

"Are you there?" I ask in a panic.

"Yeah, I'm here."

"What do you mean *arrested*?" I whisper.

"I don't have a long time to talk, Jam. They arrested us at the protest. Don't stress. They haven't charged me yet. But can you try to look up a legal aid lawyer? I don't want Dad involved. I'll tell him myself. Is Bilal around?"

"I've been trying to get in contact with him all day. He took off this morning and his phone is off."

She gives me instructions as to which station she is at and what I'm to do. I'm to search the White Pages for a local legal aid lawyer.

I flop down miserably on my bed and start biting my nails, racking my brains for a solution. I don't know who to turn to. I try Bilal's mobile again but the woman on the other end is relentless in her advice to me to "please try again later". I angrily throw my phone away.

I find the number for the local branch of legal aid. I'm greeted with a recorded message telling me that opening hours are Monday to Friday, nine to five. What do people do in these situations? The cops don't suspend their arresting powers on the weekend.

I want to scream out in frustration and then it dawns on

me so clearly that I want to jump up and down: John's father is a lawyer! It might be worth a shot to send John a message.

From: Ten_Things_I_Hate_About_Me@hotmail.com
To: Rage_Against_The_Machine@hotmail.com
URGENT URGENT URGENT URGENT JOHN, I URGENTLY NEED YOU TO REPLY TO THIS MSG. I KNOW YOU'RE THERE SO DON'T IGNORE ME. PLEASE. MY SISTER HAS BEEN ARRESTED. SHE'S AT PARRAMATTA POLICE STATION. SHE NEEDS A LAWYER AND SYDNEY DOESN'T BELIEVE IN WEEKEND JUSTICE. PLEASE REPLY. I NEED YOUR DAD'S HELP. YOU CAN CALL ME ON 042135654.

I trawl through the numbers in the White Pages, trying to find a lawyer who is available on the weekend. Only recorded messages.

Bilal's phone is still switched off too.

Finally there is movement on my computer screen. A flashing icon indicating that John has posted a reply. I open the message, my heart playing ping-pong against my stomach.

From: Rage_Against_The_Machine@hotmail.com
To: Ten_Things_I_Hate_About_Me@hotmail.com
Meet me at Parramatta police station in ½ hr.

38

I grab the stash of money I keep in my make-up box and book a taxi. Bilal's phone is still switched off and I resolve to give him a black eye when I see him next.

It takes an eternity for the taxi to arrive (well, fifteen minutes, but I feel like I've aged enough to qualify for a pension by the time I hear the beep of the horn). I instruct the driver to take me to Parramatta police station urgently. He gives me a suspicious look, which I ignore. Of course, because I'm in a hurry he decides to creep along the roads, slowing down before each traffic light just in case it turns amber. I crack my knuckles nervously. I try to withstand the powerful temptation to throw myself forward and press down on the accelerator.

We finally crawl into the right street. My hands are all clamped and sweaty, and a heavy feeling descends on me as I walk up to the doors of the police station.

John should be here soon but I can't bear another minute without seeing Shereen. I approach the front desk nervously and, in a timid voice, ask to see my sister.

"What's her name?" a Sergeant Kris Doleson asks, giving me a patronizing look. Well, who can blame her? How many people have "sister" under "given name' on their police reports?

"Shereen Towfeek."

"Wait one moment please."

She returns after several minutes. "You can't see her. She's in custody. She gets one visitor and has requested a lawyer."

I take a seat in the reception area. It's chaotic and noisy, police officers rushing in and out, people milling around, some talking loudly, others huddled together, engrossed in hushed discussions. I try to figure out if anybody looks like a lawyer. But the only exposure I've had to legal personalities has been through shows like *Law and Order* and the lawyers there are usually dressed in dark suits. The only person in business attire here is an old man dressed in a bottle-green tweed suit and hat, holding on to a string of worry beads as he speaks to a young man who is clearly related to him.

I lean my head back against the pinboard behind me and close my eyes for a moment, absorbing the noises around me. When I open them I decide to wait for John outside, hoping that it might make it easier for us to recognize each other away from the crowd of people.

I find a ledge and hop up on to it, leaning my elbow against my thigh and cupping my chin in my hand. I stare at two ants doing circles on the concrete and wonder if they're in a relationship.

Ten minutes later I hear a voice from behind me: "Hi, Jamie."

I turn around and to my bewilderment Timothy is standing there, his hands clamped down in his pockets, his face etched with nervous tension. I give him a long, searching look, not comprehending his presence.

"What are you doing here?" I ask, my voice strained and confused.

"Mum's a legal aid lawyer. . . She's just parking the car."

I'm still confused and blunder on. "But what are you doing here?"

He raises his eyebrows slowly and hunches his shoulders up, seemingly waiting for me to understand. And in a second it dawns on me. The truth hits me so hard that I almost lose my balance on the ledge. I suck in a deep breath to stop my insides from disintegrating like sand dunes washed into nothingness by a violent wave.

My eyes widen in shock. "No. . ." I whisper in horror.

He nods slowly, painfully, never once turning his gaze from me. "I'm sorry . . . I didn't mean to deceive you. . ."

I raise my hand, cutting him off midway through his sentence. "You're *John*? You've been *John* all along?"

He nods and I wince, as though defending myself from the cuts of a knife.

"Why didn't you say something?"

"I wanted to but I chickened out."

I'm too numb to yell and shout. Anyway, there isn't a chance because a woman walks up to us from the kerb, a folder wedged under her armpit. She's tall like Timothy and dressed in slacks and a shirt. Her hair is tied back into a low ponytail and her face is bare except for a touch of lipstick.

She stands before me and smiles warmly. "Hi, Jamie, I'm Sandra. Timothy's told me a lot about you. I'm sorry to hear about your sister. Shall we go in and see what the story is?"

The words have been sucked right out of me. I open my mouth. Nothing.

So I nod slowly and hop off the ledge. As we walk to the doors I remember my manners. I force myself to speak and turn to Sandra and thank her for coming.

"Not a problem," she says. "I used to be an avid protestor myself in my university days."

I give her a half-smile and turn my head away, averting my face from Timothy's gaze.

Sandra instructs Timothy and I to wait in the lobby while she sees her "client". The word hits me hard. It affirms Shereen's induction into that group of Australians who have been arrested. I'd always joked about this and it was always my father's deepest anxiety. For once his paranoia wasn't misguided.

I take a seat and Timothy has the sense to choose a seat across from me, rather than fill the empty one next to me. He leans forward, then seems to think twice, and leans back. Then he leans forward again, running his fingers through his hair, and says nervously: "Let me explain, Jamie."

"I don't want to talk about it now," I say coldly.

"But—"

"No," I cut him off.

He doesn't continue and leans back.

I reach into my pocket and take out my mobile, trying Bilal's number again. It's finally ringing and Bilal eventually answers.

"Where have you been?" I yell.

"I was helping my mate fix his car, why?"

"Shereen's been arrested—"

"*What?*"

"I don't know why, something about a protest. We're at Parramatta police station. Can you please come now?"

"I'm in the car as we speak. I should be there in twenty. Does Dad know?"

"No! Of course not!"

"All right. I'll see you soon. Stop stressing, OK, Jam?"

My chin starts to quiver but I force myself, with every

brain cell and inch of will power, to stop myself from crying. "Yeah, OK."

I hang up and Timothy looks at me with concern. I ignore him and fumble with the zipper on my bag. Up and down, down and up. I'm sure the rest of the people in the reception area are ready to pounce on me in annoyance.

Several minutes of silence passes when Timothy suddenly says: "I wonder if there's a phobia of police stations."

I ignore his conciliatory smile and respond with my filthiest, most obnoxious look. "Very funny. You're a natural."

"I had no idea to begin with. I'm sorry."

"You completely betrayed me. I wouldn't even know where to start! I opened up to *John* about everything—"

"I never told any—"

"That's beside the point! What right did you have? You knew that I was revealing my deepest secrets to somebody I thought was a stranger! And you didn't even tell me!"

"If you hadn't been so self-centred, you would have worked it out! It was there for you to see. And when you didn't work it out I blocked your email."

"Seriously, shut up. Just shut up. There is nothing you can say to make this better." I stand up and storm out of the reception area.

"Where are you going?" he calls out.

"I'm going to wait outside for my brother, Bilal. Oh, but you know his name is Bilal, don't you? You know all about him!"

238

I turn on my heels and walk out, resuming my position on the ledge. When Bilal arrives I answer his barrage of questions and then we go inside and wait.

I'm tempted to ask Bilal to bash up Timothy, the way it happens in the movies. Protect my honour, stick up for me, that kind of thing.

This is the kind of totally stupid and violent fantasy I'm entertaining as I wait to know if my sister is going to forever be known as a convicted felon. I suppose, technically, an arrest over a peace rally won't amount to that, but that's what people like Uncle Joseph will say if they find out.

We're sitting in the reception area and I'm ignoring Timothy, despite the fact that his mother is here helping Shereen. That presents a dilemma. I should probably introduce him to Bilal.

"Bilal, this is Timothy," I half grunt. "His mum is a lawyer and she's inside helping Shereen."

"G'day, mate," Bilal says, leaning over and shaking Timothy's hand. "Thanks for your help."

"No problem." Timothy glances at me but I ignore him.

"School friend?" Bilal asks me in Arabic.

"Not a friend, just an acquaintance," I reply in Arabic. Timothy looks at us inquisitively and I raise my eyebrows at him as if to say, *you-don't-understand-us-na-na-na-na-na*. Completely childish, I know.

Bilal looks at me suspiciously. "Are you sure? He keeps staring at you."

"He's mentally deranged."

"Then what hope is there with his mum?"

"She seems fine. Besides, we need whoever we can get."

"He looks like he does pot. *Does he do pot?*"

"No, he gets high on tropical fish."

"Is that a new drug?" Bilal asks, confused.

It's been two hours and forty-five minutes since I first arrived at the police station. My bum is numb from sitting on the plastic chair. I look over at Timothy, who is sitting with his legs stretched out, his head leaning back against the wall as he listens to his iPod. It occurs to me that he doesn't have to be here. That he could have left a long time ago. But I quickly light a match to that thought. I'm in no mood for feeling an ounce of appreciation or gratitude towards him. The shock and humiliation are still too raw.

Sandra finally emerges. Walking behind her is Shereen. I'm expecting to see her in handcuffs and zebra-striped jumpsuit. I wonder if they'd make her wear a zebra-striped hijab. I've watched way too many movies.

Shereen looks as normal as ever. White Yin Yang patched hijab, a scarf in the colours of the Iraqi flag wrapped around her shoulders, long-sleeved T-shirt with *SILENCE IS CONSENT* written over it, jeans and brown Blundstones. She grins at Bilal and me and rushes over. It's group hug time.

I remember Timothy and Sandra. I turn around and thank Sandra.

"No problem. They didn't lay any charges so everything's fine from here. We can all go home now."

"What do we owe you?" Bilal asks.

"Nothing!" she cries, dismissing his question with a wave of her hand.

"No, seriously," Shereen says, stepping in. "I owe you something. I've taken up your whole afternoon."

Sandra smiles. "I did this because Timothy asked me as a special favour. He said it was for a close friend. So please, don't spoil it with talk of money. Consider it my contribution to civil rights." She chuckles and Shereen gives her a warm hug.

Timothy is standing awkwardly beside his mother.

"Thanks. . ." I mutter uncomfortably.

"No problem," he mutters back.

We leave the police station. Shereen is gushing out praise and thanks over Timothy's valiancy in coming to her aid. I want to take her aside and quietly inform her that he is an email imposter who tricked me into telling him all about our lives.

I jump into the back seat of Bilal's car and we drive off to Parramatta for a quick coffee and debriefing session before we return home.

It's now five o'clock and I suddenly remember that I've been out of the house for an entire day without Dad knowing or having even called. So I send him a text message and tell him that I'm with Shereen and Bilal in Parramatta.

He sends one back: *Nex tim you ask befre you lev the hose.*

I don't have much in the way of a rebuttal argument so I reply: *OK.*

We choose a table outside a café on Church Street. Shereen proceeds to tell us what happened.

"We were trying to make a bit of noise as a procession of government officials and MPs were arriving at the entrance of Parliament House. It got out of hand. Some idiot started to burn the flag. I rushed over with Cam and Tisha to try and get him to stop. Of course the cameras started rolling at that point. Then he started throwing stuff at the cops. Bottles and cans. The cops came in hard and we got caught up in it all."

"So was it worth it?" I ask.

Shereen stares at the table, fiddling with a packet of Sweet'N Low. A moment's pause. Cars drive past. The traffic light turns red. A yellow Porsche revs its engine for our benefit. The steady hum of conversation and laughter surrounds us.

She looks up and our eyes connect. "I still think silence is consent. But I realized something whilst sitting in the holding cell, wondering whether I'd end up in jail. Despite the fact that I've been screaming and shouting and venting, I think my voice got lost. There are only so many causes you can champion. I was all rhetoric." She pauses, tapping her fingers on the table. "I need a focus."

"So what now?" Bilal asks.

"This will probably sound really sanctimonious—"

"Ahem!" Bilal says. "English please!"

Shereen smiles. "Stuck up."

"So say stuck up instead of using a word that has every letter of the alphabet."

Shereen and I groan.

"Anyway," Shereen continues, "I want to try and make an impact at the grass roots level of society. You know, reach out to communities who feel isolated and alienated. I want to help them feel connected. And besides, we need more diversity in the police force."

Bilal slams his hands down on the table and bursts out laughing. "A cop? That's awesome!"

Shereen grins. "Of course, I could never do any undercover assignments. Unless it's investigating the beef content in a kebab at Lakemba."

"I wonder what Dad will say."

"He'll probably think it's too dangerous for a girl," Bilal says, rolling his eyes.

"Actually I'm pretty optimistic that he'll be OK with my decision. I think he'll be happy that I've finally worked out what I want to do with my life."

"I'm not so optimistic," Bilal says.

"What do you mean?" I ask.

"I got a job."

Shereen and I squeal with excitement. *"Really?"*

"An apprenticeship with a top mechanic. Not exactly Dad's ideal job description for me."

"It's fantastic!" Shereen cries.

"Yeah! You're finally going to get off your arse and do something with your life," I tease. "Think of all those poor bimbos you'll no longer have time for."

He hits me playfully on the shoulder. "You never have nothing positive to contribute do you, Jam?"

"Double negatives, Bilal."

"And I'm *still* hot and sexy."

Shereen and I groan.

"So does Dad know yet?" I ask.

"Nope. I'll tell him when he's in a good mood."

Shereen lets out a short laugh. "What happened today is going to ensure that window of opportunity is closed for the next thirty-five years."

We arrive home an hour later. Dad is sitting on the back verandah, smoking his *argeela* and reading a book of Arabic poetry. Each of us greets him with a kiss on the top of his head. No words of anger pass between Bilal and Dad. Just a kiss, a gruff "Hi" and an uncomfortable few words about their day. It's how they always make up and move on. Without acknowledging the past. Without talking about the future. Just quiet recognition that this is how it is and family goes on.

Shereen motions for Bilal and me to go inside. She has some confessing to do.

Bilal and I sit in the lounge room, each of us taking turns to eavesdrop.

At first he yells. About the shame. About the

consequences. About police records and future job applications and community gossip.

And then she speaks. About ideals and dreams and naivety. About mistakes and understanding and forgiveness and the future.

And then there is silence. We sneak a look outside.

There is no longer any talking.

Just a long hug between two people who are learning to understand each other a little more.

39

"**W**indow of opportunity," Shereen hisses at Bilal as she passes us in the hallway later on in the week. We respond with blank expressions.

"Apprenticeship. Good mood. Dad." Her voice is hushed as her eyes scan the end of the hallway for a sign of Dad. "Something must have happened at madrasa. He's home on a high."

"How do you know?" Bilal asks.

She looks at us calmly and then smiles. "He just suggested that I take Jamilah to the movies. I quote: *She's been cooped up at home and seems down lately*. As you are both aware, it is past sunset. It is a week night. Jamilah being cooped up has never concerned him in the past."

"Oh God! Dad's gone senile!" I fan my face with my hand, trying to calm myself down.

"Maybe somebody slipped something into his coffee at madrasa," Bilal suggests.

"Whatever the reason," Shereen says impatiently, "just get your butt into the lounge room and talk to him."

Bilal runs his fingers nervously through his hair. "OK, I'm going."

"And Bilal," Shereen says, gently touching his arm, "don't lose your temper."

Shereen turns to me when Bilal has disappeared inside the lounge room. "Positions?"

"I'll take the kitchen door. You take the hallway. We'll regroup in the bathroom."

Bilal's never been subtle or diplomatic. He's as smooth as whipped cream on the dance floor or on the phone with a girl. But put him in a room with Dad and the cream curdles.

He walks into the lounge room, sits down on a chair and leans forward. "I've got an apprenticeship, Dad. Are you gunna give me a hard time about it or be happy for me?"

I lean backwards and my eyes connect with Shereen's. She has a horrified expression on her face. She pretends to cut her throat and I pretend to strangle myself. We go back to our positions.

"Is it a full-time position?"

"Yes."

"A good garage?"

"Yes. One of the best. It won some small-business awards."

"So there's room to move up?"

I can just make out Bilal's face from where I'm standing. He's been caught completely off guard. His face is twisted with confusion. I lean back again and Shereen looks my way. She throws her hands in the air and shrugs. I shake my head, completely bewildered too.

"Dave — he's the guy who owns the joint — said that if I stick with him I could manage one of his franchises."

"And this is what you want? This is what you've decided to make of your future?"

"Yes." Bilal sits up tall and defiant. "This is what I want for *my* life."

"Then may Allah listen to the prayers of a father and bless you, Bilal. May he make this decision the start of a successful life."

Bilal is momentarily speechless. He stands up and stares at Dad. "Er . . . thanks, Dad."

Dad looks up at him and nods.

The three of us meet in the bathroom. We look at each other with dazed expressions. And then slowly we start to grin.

Amy isn't at school for three consecutive days. She hasn't replied to my text messages or answered my missed calls on her mobile. I send a text to Liz, asking her if she's heard from Amy. I don't receive a reply.

"Do you know what's going on with Amy?" I ask in homeroom.

"No idea," she says, blowing a bubble with her chewing gum. She leans in close. "So has he asked you yet?"

"Huh?"

"Sam told me Peter's going to ask you to the formal," she whispers through clenched lips. "It's only three weeks away. Can you believe it? The most popular guy is going to ask you to the formal! It will be so cool! We can double date!"

"I'm worried about Amy. She's been missing school a lot lately."

Liz is not amused. "Didn't you hear me? Peter might ask you out."

"That's nice," I say in a distracted tone, "but don't you think something might be up with Amy?"

"How long has she been away from school?"

"Haven't you noticed?"

She lets out an embarrassed burst of laughter. "Not really, to tell you the truth. We're not that close any more. I think she's jealous."

"Of what?"

She almost looks offended and then seems to take pity on me. She stares at me with the resolve of somebody about to educate the ignorant. "She's jealous of my relationship with Sam and the fact that I'm with the in-crowd now. She's probably jealous that Peter's interested in you too. He likes you because you're quiet. It doesn't have to go too deep, you know? You can have your fun without any complications."

Without any complications.

I'm beginning to realize that I want complications. I need

them. Because without them I'm a shadow in the playground. A whisper in the classroom. Barely here or there. I'm not living. I'm just surviving. Surviving a battle of my own making.

Peter is all arrogance and good looks. He grins at me and his confidence is maddening.

"So is it a date?"

For the first time in my life I realize that I deserve more. But I'm not quite ready to admit that I'm not allowed to go to the formal. I make a promise to myself: this will be my last lie.

"Thanks for asking me. But I already have a date."

My words impact on him like a car airbag exploding in somebody's face. His forehead twists in confusion. His eyes widen in surprise.

"*You* have a date? Who?"

"It's a surprise."

40

I have my confrontation with Timothy in the playground at McDonald's as I'm cleaning up the remains of a squashed junior burger and soft-serve cone off the slippery slide.

I'm clearing the table in the playground when a little girl with a mane of golden hair and bright brown eyes walks up to me. She informs me that I have an "ugly uniform", and looks me in the eye as she proceeds to mix her burger and cone on the slide. The temptation to dress her in the ice cream is overwhelming. Her mother storms over and demands that I clean it up before it poses a public liability risk to other children.

It's times like these that I start to question the value of my emancipation.

As I'm scraping the gooey mess into a paper towel I feel a tap on my shoulder.

It's Timothy.

"It's not good to play with your food," he jokes.

I give him a look that clearly indicates I'm not amused and stand up, a soggy mess of paper towels in one gloved hand, a bottle of disinfectant in the other.

"You're holding that disinfectant like it's a can of mace. You hate me that much, hey?"

"Let's see," I say, "you only pretended to be somebody else all this time. You read my innermost thoughts when you knew I didn't want a soul at school to know about my life. You deceived me."

"I never deceived you. Not once did I lie to you. Emailing you was a coincidence. At first I had no idea it was you. I never hid who I was. It was right there for you to see if you'd only opened your eyes."

"That's no excuse! There you were telling me to be true to myself and to be honest and upfront and blah blah blah. What a load of crap when all along it was you who was the phoney."

We've developed a bit of an audience. A couple of children are standing around us now, oohing and ahhing at the "grown-ups fighting".

"I guess that's it then," he says, shrugging his shoulders. "I'll see you around."

He turns on his heels and walks to the purple and red gate.

He can't slam the gate in anger because it has a childproof lock, and who would slam a gate which has a smiling picture of Ronald McDonald painted on it? I can't even cross my arms over my chest because I have ice cream melting down one hand and a kid tugging on my pants, asking me to move out of the way as I'm blocking the slide.

What an undignified mess we're in.

It doesn't take long for Uncle Joseph to find out about Shereen. Don't ask me how. It's a somebody who knows somebody who saw somebody who tells somebody kind of thing.

My father's mobile rings and I hear him answer it from his bedroom and greet Uncle Joseph. I tiptoe to the half-open door and listen carefully, watching my dad stand at his bedroom window as he talks on the phone.

"Yes, I know... No charges were laid. Yes ... well I suppose there will be people who will see it as a disgrace... Well yes, there will be men who will lose interest now... Yes, Joseph, yes ... thank you for telling me ... Jamilah? Oh yes, she's still working ... yes I'm still letting her... As far as I know she does not smoke, it's just some extra pocket money... Oh well, Bilal's found a job and he's very excited... No, he won't be going to university... I understand that you care... Goodbye."

I let out a heavy sigh. Once again my father has failed to come to our rescue. Uncle Joseph continues to preach and my father takes every blow, leaving Shereen, Bilal and me to deal with the long-lasting bruises.

My dad is staring out the window. He then sits on the edge of his bed and puts his head in his hands. I can sense the weariness oozing out of him, like air being slowly released from a balloon. I'm transfixed, watching him deflate like that. Then he suddenly sits up straight, grabs his mobile phone and dials.

"Joseph," he says in a firm tone. "Yes, I'm well thank you. . . Yes, something is wrong . . . I don't appreciate you calling me and saying such things about my children. Jamilah's proven herself to be responsible. I have every faith in her. And Shereen's intentions have always been noble and sincere. She's learned her lesson. She's only ever made me worry because she has too much heart. As for Bilal, he's exceptionally talented at what he does and I know he will go far.

"No, you listen to me, Joseph, I'm not concerned with how it looks or what people will say. . . No, hear me out. I trust my girls. This society is full of temptation but my daughters are always making me proud. Do you understand, Joseph? That is all *you* and anybody else who wishes to talk needs to know. . . Yes . . . we will see each other soon, *Inshallah,* God willing. Goodbye, Joseph."

I remember my dad giving us piggyback rides through the house and my mother yelling at him to be careful because I'd be laughing so hard I'd be half dangling off his back. I remember him peeling every inch of the white pulp from my mandarins and dividing them into segments for me. I remember the way his eyes light up when he recounts lifting me from my mother's stomach during her Caesarean operation.

I remember all these things and they glide around in my head like ballroom dancers.

I have one more memory to add now. And that's Dad telling Uncle Joseph he is proud of me.

41

My father calls a family meeting. Bilal, Shereen and I take our seats in the living room and my dad sits in his armchair, clutching on to his water-pipe as though it were a life-support system.

"Bilal, Shereen, Jamilah," he starts, his voice shaky. He clears his throat and continues. "You all know I love your mother very much. She was and always will be my first love. She is the mother of my children. May Allah rest her soul and grant her paradise. . . It's been seven years now and not a day goes by when I don't think of her. Not a day will go by when I will not think of her."

He doesn't need to finish. It hits me hard. I pre-empt him and blurt out: "You've met somebody! You're getting married!"

He looks at me in surprise. I see his fingers wrap themselves tighter over the pipe.

"Yes, Jamilah." He looks down at his lap. At first I'm confused by his demeanour. My father has never sought our approval or counsel about matters to do with him. Indeed, he has rarely sought our opinion about matters to do with us. For the first time he seems vulnerable. So open and approachable.

"I have . . . met somebody who I. . ." he clears his throat, raising his eyes to glance at each of us in turn, ". . .wish to marry. She is a good woman. In fact, she is practically part of our family already. I have asked Sajda for her hand in marriage and she has accepted."

The three of us look at one another in mute shock. The announcement is met with drawn breaths, heads in hands, stunned silence.

The betrayal slices through me. It cuts into me, dices me, chops me up into tiny pieces. I confided in her. I allowed myself to trust that she cared about me. But now it seems it was all for an ulterior purpose. To get close to me. Gain my trust and then slide right in.

My dad sighs. "Please try to understand. Sajda will never replace your mother. It is impossible. But people need companionship."

Bilal clears his throat and makes to say something but then stops. He leans back in his chair, the words seeming to recoil in his throat.

Bilal and I look at Shereen, our eyes pleading with her to

257

come to the rescue. She stands up slowly and approaches my dad.

"Don't worry about our reaction, Dad. It will take getting used to, that's all." She embraces him in a big hug.

Bilal follows her lead and kisses my dad. "*Mabruk.* Congratulations, Dad." He steps aside and I lean down and hug my father. I stupidly burst into tears and he hugs me tighter.

42

Anger works in mysterious ways. It can keep you awake all night whispering ugly words to you. It can rumble away in your stomach, sapping the energy from you, leaving you distracted and irritable. It almost always becomes irrational as it builds up inside you.

I plot and I plan. I pace my room. I curl up silently into my pillow. I avoid eye contact with my dad. I stick to small talk. I pretend to be busy with homework. I don't want him to know how I'm feeling. I don't want to hurt him. I vent with Bilal and Shereen. But Bilal thinks it will be a good thing. "Maybe he'll relax more. He's got nothing to do except be a parent. Let him be a husband again and get off our backs for a while."

I turn to Shereen for support. She's thought long and hard about it. Cried into her pillow. Sat like a zombie in her room. Spent hours on the phone with Aunt Sowsan. One morning I wake up to find her sitting on the edge of my bed.

"Mum was sweet," she says. "But Jamilah, she wasn't perfect. We all have this romantic, idealized memory of her. Well, you know what I think? I think that initially she wouldn't have wanted Dad to remarry."

"Really?"

"I remember she was the jealous type. She used to give Dad a hard time whenever he talked to our old neighbour, Gloria. The girl with the boob job and stilettos under her robe. Remember?"

My memories are of playing football in the street, skateboarding on our front lawn and avoiding Mr Sinclair, who barked at us whenever we made too much noise.

"You were too young. Anyway, I have this feeling she'd have wanted Dad to wait. But not for ever. She would have wanted him to have a second chance at happiness. I'm certain of that. So I don't think we're betraying her by supporting Dad. I think she'd be disappointed if we didn't."

But I'm still angry. I'm angry with Miss Sajda. And I'm angry with myself. Because I realize that I'm selfish. I'm no longer concerned that I'll be a traitor to my mother for standing by my father. If anybody knew Mum, it was Shereen. I trust her when she says that Mum would approve. What I'm concerned about is how my life will change. A new woman in the house. A new adult authority. Will I lose a devoted father? Will my dad become stricter? Will he stop speaking about my mother? Will I have to take the photographs of my mother and father down from my walls and dressing table? Will I be expected to take orders from Miss Sajda? Will she change? Will she defer to my father's strict rules and forget about my feelings?

Each thought adds a further brick to my house of anger. The foundation is laid. The cement between each brick dries.

I'm quiet at madrasa today. I'm all monosyllables and moodiness. I scribble in the corner of my notebook, ignoring Miss Sajda's lecture on the difference between masculine and feminine pronouns.

Class finishes and Mustafa, Samira and Hasan start removing their instruments in preparation for rehearsal. I tell them I'm not staying back today. Miss Sajda looks at me in surprise and asks to see me alone outside.

I step outside. I lean my back against a pole, fold my arms across my chest and stare at her.

"I've been meaning to come and give you a hug," she says, smiling warmly at me. "We're going to be family. I want you to know, Jamilah, that I am in love with your father. He's a breath of fresh air in my life. I wanted to tell you but I left it for him to decide when he was ready to let you all know."

"You used me."

She recoils, clearly shocked. "*Used* you?"

"Yes. You pretended to be my friend. Somebody I could open up to. All along you were trying to score points. Make some kind of impression with me. It was for all the wrong reasons."

"Jamilah! How can you say that? I never wanted to hurt you or use you. You needed somebody to talk to and I wanted to be there for you."

"Why? So you could get through to my dad?"

I'm hurting her. I can see it in her eyes. The wider they get, the more pain seeps in.

"Do you think I'm that insincere?" I turn my eyes from her. "When will you learn to trust people?"

"I trusted you!"

"You don't trust anyone. If you did you'd be upfront at school. You would trust that your closest friend and classmates would respect you for the person you are, not the stereotype you imagine yourself to be. You would trust yourself! Trust that you're strong enough to stand up to people like Peter."

"This isn't about Amy or Peter or school! Don't replay what I've confided in you to make your point."

"It has everything to do with it. It's about you and how you deal with people. When it comes to giving me the benefit of the doubt, you don't have enough faith in me to trust that I truly care for you. Do you really think so little of yourself, Jamilah, that you would think somebody would only befriend you for an ulterior motive?"

She takes a step towards me. She stares at me. Into me. I feel transparent. As thin and fragile as a tissue flapping in the wind. There is so much understanding in her eyes. The anger pent up inside me crumbles. It is not designed to handle truth. I know that she can see the girl crouched inside me. She can see the longing in my eyes. The longing to break free.

I've never held myself accountable for my actions. I've cried into my pillow, wondering why Amy won't open up to me. I've been so self-centred, expecting to take without giving. Timothy's right. If I had just opened my eyes I would have realized who "John" was. I was so busy hiding who I was from everyone, including myself, that I was completely unaware of anyone else.

It's easier to think the worst of people. You become a martyr to yourself. A victim of your assumptions. There's no need to build relationships with others when you have such low expectations. But it leaves you alone. And I'm tired of being alone.

"I'm sorry to have doubted you."

She takes another step towards me. And I take the next, meeting her halfway, at the point where faith replaces mistrust and high expectations bring out the best in us.

43

I spend Saturday morning cleaning the house with Shereen. We dust, mop and disinfect every crack and corner. Thankfully, Bilal's room is strictly out of bounds. Shereen even washes the curtains, ignoring my protests that they won't dry in time (it's more the fact that I can't be bothered hanging them on the washing line). Bilal and Dad are in the back and front yards, pruning the hedges, mowing the lawn and tidying up the outdoor seating area.

The manic cleaning is attributable to a special occasion at our house tonight. My father and Miss Sajda will recite the *fatiha*, the first chapter from the Koran, to formally announce and bless their intentions of marrying. My dad will then present Miss Sajda with jewellery and gifts. Aunt

Sowsan and Uncle Ameen are also invited and my dad has planned a feast.

My dad has insisted that none of us, including Aunt Sowsan, cooks. Instead, he has ordered a lamb to roast on a spit and organized salads and various other dishes from a Lebanese caterer. He's also arranged for trays of Arabic sweets to be delivered from a nearby patisserie. So there will be no pots and pans to wash and that keeps me humming merrily as I attend to my chores.

I still have mixed feelings about the whole thing. A part of me feels that being happy for my dad will somehow betray my mother's memory. It's a part of me that refuses to share this house with another woman. I can't bear to think that there will be somebody else in the kitchen my mother cooked in, the lounge room she sat in, the hallway she walked in. Her fingerprints are everywhere and it's as though Miss Sajda's presence will rub them away for ever. It's not that Miss Sajda is the wrong person. It could be anyone. I would still be dealing with this gnawing uncertainty in the pit of my stomach.

Shereen tells me our mother would understand. "Dad waited seven years, Jamilah," she says. "There were times he refused to even contemplate remarrying and argued with his friends. But we'll leave this house one day and he'll be alone. He deserves a second chance too."

Aunt Sowsan insists that Miss Sajda would never dream of taking our mother's place.

Their words are reassuring. They wrap around me like a

warm blanket on a cold day. But just as there are moments of warmth, there are moments, underneath that blanket, when I find myself shivering and my teeth chattering. Maybe it will never be one emotion for me. Maybe life was never meant to be constant. I'll have to deal with this new life and feel love and hate and annoyance and excitement and fear and courage many times over.

Dinner is typically colourful: everybody speaking over the top of each other, raucous laughter, Arabic jokes I don't understand, Aunt Sowsan force-feeding us seconds and thirds, Shereen and I ganging up on Bilal when it comes time to clear the dishes.

And then there's Dad and "Aunt" Sajda. The "aunt" is going to take practice. Throughout the night I see my dad take such pains to ensure that she has enough food on her plate, that her glass is never empty, that she is relaxed, that Shereen, Bilal and I converse with her and make her feel at home.

After dinner, Miss Sajda bumps into me in the hallway, on her way to the bathroom. She smiles self-consciously at me and I smile back. There's an awkward pause and I look down at the floor.

"I know this must be strange to you," Miss Sajda says. "Jamilah, I just want to make your father happy. But I want to do that as his second wife, not as a replacement for his first, your mother, *Alayirhamha*. Please trust me."

And I do.

Shortly after dessert we all sit down in the lounge room.

During the recitation of the *fatiha* we ask God to bless my father and Miss Sajda's commitment to each other. A lot of thoughts float through my mind. Most of them petty. I find myself wondering whether Miss Sajda will understand that I only use triple fluoride toothpaste and that Dad prefers Nescafé Gold Blend over Blend 43. I wonder whether I'll have to endure a Saturday morning ritual of spring-cleaning, whether she will interfere with my television viewing routine and whether she'll be able to convince my father to quit smoking.

I find myself wondering about all these tiny, silly things at a time when I probably should be reflecting on the meaning of life, the power of God and love and the tender way my dad presents Miss Sajda with a gift set of jewellery.

But then, as the night draws on and I see my dad's wrinkled forehead stretch out in laughter and the creases around his eyes crinkle whenever he catches Miss Sajda's eyes and smiles affectionately at her, I find myself wondering something else: how could I ever deny him the joy of no longer feeling lonely?

44

I don't want to sound like a whinger. Maybe you think the whole Who Am I? identity question is about as interesting as a biology assignment on the mating habits of blue-tongued lizards. But listen up. It's the type of question that can keep me awake at night as I stare at moving shadows on my wall and pretend that they're ghosts dancing at a nightclub. It's the kind of question that makes me feel like a berry in a jar of Fruits of the Forest jam who wonders what burst of goodness and flavour she'll bring to the whole jam and toast experience.

All I want to know is what place I have in this country I call home. It all comes down to emotional real estate. Finding your place, renovating it as you go along (a haircut here, a university degree there), and having neighbourly relations with other property owners.

So far, I've figured that dyeing my hair blonde, poking my eyes out with contact lenses and living a lie at school all guarantee me a share in the Australian property market. But I'm starting to realize how empty my bit of "place" is. It's got no soul. The cosmetics are fantastic and would look great on domain.com. But you can't smell life. It tastes like stale Ryvita biscuits and sounds like socks on carpet.

So I think I'm going to do something about it. I'm going to fix things with Amy. I'm going to forgive Timothy. And I'm going to risk it all and play in the band.

I call Amy on Sunday morning and invite her over.

She rings the doorbell three hours later. Bilal, who is washing his car in the carport and admiring his chest in his side mirrors, yells out at me through the window to answer the door. I open the door and Amy is standing on the porch.

"Your brother?"

"Unfortunately."

"*Hot*," she whispers, grinning at me.

"Shh! He might hear you and then I'll be forced to hire a crane to help his neck support his big head."

She steps in and I take a deep breath. My identity colours every wall, decorates every corner. But I'm ready for this. I'm ready to trust.

I lead her to my bedroom. We pass the Koranic

inscriptions hanging on the walls. The *argeela* sitting in the hallway corner. My dad has the radio playing loudly in the background, sounding out Arabic folk songs.

She throws her shoes off, sits down on my bed and crosses her legs underneath her. We go through my CD collection and my father knocks on my bedroom door.

He's been working in his veggie patch in the garden and his tartan shirt and faded grey tracksuit pants with the tight ankle elastic and his masseur slippers are flecked with soil. As he steps into my room I get a whiff of mint – he has mint leaves lodged in his hair.

"This is Amy. From school."

"Hi," she says.

My father smiles warmly at her and says, in his thick accent: "It so lovely to having one of Jamilah's friends here in our house! Jamilah never bringing her friend here. Welcome!"

He says my name and I look uneasily at Amy, wondering if she's noticed.

"Thanks," she says, looking up and smiling brightly at my father. "Have you been gardening?"

"Yes, I looking very, how to say. . .?" He looks down at his clothes and looks up at us, a grin on his face. "Armano Versaco. . .?"

"Oh boy," I moan, throwing my face in my hands.

"Anyway, I leave you both. Jamilah looking like she swallowing a cockroach. I knowing when adult no welcome."

"Thanks, Dad," I say, rolling my eyes.

"I go back to my vegetables. They no talk back to me or rolling their eyes."

"*Dad!*"

He chuckles, clearly enjoying my reddening face. "Amy, you stay for dinner? We order pizza, OK?"

"Thanks. That would be nice."

"You are the first friend I meet of Jamilah, would you believe?"

"*Dad*," I mutter. "Can we have some privacy now please?"

"Yes, yes, OK."

"He can be a bit of a dag at times," I say, when he leaves the room.

"He seems nice. . . So do you want to watch a DVD? Or watch your brother wash his car?"

I throw a cushion at her. "Yuk! Get over him please! I'll help you out. He leaves the toilet seat up, never picks his wet towels off the floor and burps at the table. Anyway . . . that's not why I invited you over."

"I guess perving at your brother wouldn't be a motivation for you."

"I invited you over because. . ." I pause and take a deep breath. "You're going to hate me. . ." I look down at my lap and wring my hands nervously.

"What is it?"

"I've been . . . lying to you. I've never been upfront with you, Amy. All this time I've tried to hide my identity because I've been so worried about how people would judge me."

"Judge you? Why?"

"This is going to sound so dumb. . ."

"Go on."

"I'm Lebanese-Muslim. My name's Jamilah, not Jamie." I slump down into my chair and groan, my face hidden by my hands. "I've been hiding myself for a long time."

I can't believe I've admitted it out loud. The relief floods through me but is instantly swept away by panic. Panic that Amy will no longer want to be my friend. I look over at her, shamefaced, hoping she won't despise me for it.

"So what?"

I've spent so long predicting her reaction that her rejection of me is permanently imprinted in my mind, like a hand print in wet concrete. I stare at her, open-mouthed, not daring to think I might have been wrong. "Huh?"

"I don't get it. Why would you hide that from me when it's no big deal?"

So I explain it to her. Paint her a picture of my world. A world of headlines and documentaries and summits and bad press. A world of stereotypes and generalizations. A world in which I'm a perfect target for Peter's racist game of archery. And she looks at me calmly and asks what any of that has to do with her.

I fumble around for the right words. How do you tell somebody that you were foolish enough to think them shallow? It doesn't go down too well. In fact, she's outraged.

"Do you really think I'm that superficial?"

"I'm sorry, OK? I was afraid and it was easier to think everybody would respond in the same way."

As soon as I say it I realize how misguided I've been. I've been so afraid of people's generalizations. But I've been just as guilty of making my own.

"If you knew me well enough, you'd know I'd never be that unfair."

"It's not like we've ever been close," I say defensively. "Until Liz became glued to Sam, I always felt like the third wheel with you both."

"That's because you were constantly blowing us off every time we made plans to go out."

"I didn't want you to know that I'm not allowed to go out. My dad's really strict. I felt embarrassed to admit it."

"So all those times you cancelled and backed out, it was because you weren't allowed?"

". . .Yes."

"And you couldn't tell me that?"

I shrug my shoulders. "I didn't want you and Liz to assume it was because I was some poor, oppressed Lebanese-Muslim girl. I'm so over that stereotype."

Her face tenses up and she takes in a deep breath. "Is that the type of person you think *I* am?"

"I'm sorry. . ."

"Well I'm *not* that shallow."

"It took a while for me to wake up to myself and realize that."

"Why didn't you invite Liz?"

"Because it didn't take a long time for me to realize that she is."

She sighs heavily, absent-mindedly opening and closing a CD case lying on my bed. "Forget her. She's changed. And why? To be with a guy who goes into hysterics over Peter farting in somebody's face."

"I could have been like that."

"What? You'd fart in somebody's face?"

She grins at me and her magnanimity in the face of my unfair assumptions overwhelms me.

"I could have been like Liz. How many times did Peter make fun of Ahmed and the others? I didn't say anything."

"You shouldn't be ashamed of who you are," she says. "And stuff Peter. He has the intelligence of cardboard. Look at Ahmed, Danielle, Paul. They don't let anybody make them feel inferior."

Honesty is liberating. And tough. And worth it. It's weights and bricks and cement blocks off your shoulders. It's an orthopaedic remedy. You can suddenly stand straight and tall again. I tell Amy everything because I'm learning to trust again. I tell her my complete family history. My mother dying. My father changing. The good times with him. And the bad. Miss Sajda and new beginnings. I tell her that Shereen has a heart and conscience larger than she can sometimes bear. That Bilal's full of double negatives and bad grammar but nobody can fix an engine the way he can or stands by his sisters in the way he does. I tell her about not being allowed to go to the formal. And about the band.

"You should still play!"

"I'm going to . . . but please don't tell anybody at school. About anything. . ."

"When will you be yourself?"

"When I'm ready. Swear you won't tell anyone? I need time."

She shakes her head, clearly disappointed. "Time for what?"

"I trust you. I need to learn how to trust in myself. Swear? Please?"

"OK, I swear . . . Jamilah."

I smile. "I don't look like a Jamie, do I?"

She gives me a cheeky grin. "Come to think of it, no, you don't."

"Peroxide and blue contacts. Not exactly Jamilah material, hey?"

"Well you always forgot the eyebrows. Crucial mistake."

We laugh. Big fat belly laughs. Ones that sing inside of you like sopranos high on Gatorade.

"Can I ask you something?" I say when we've regained our breath.

"Shoot."

"Why have you been so sad lately?"

Give and take. I'm down on my knees, working hard to try to move those parallel train tracks. Twisting and shifting the metal to make them intersect. Meet halfway.

She looks at me in surprise and shrugs. "Just . . . stuff."

I won't have it. I won't have us running in the same

direction on different tracks any more. "What kind of stuff?" I press. "Is it family?"

She nods slowly.

"Why couldn't you open up to me?"

"We've never discussed family before. Actually, we've never really discussed anything meaningful."

"I hate that."

"Me too."

"I need some meaning."

"Me too."

"So what's going on?"

She sighs deeply and cups her chin in her hands, leaning her elbows against her thighs.

"You're not the only one with image pressures. I've been worried about how people will react when they know that I now come from a broken home."

"*Broken?*"

"My parents have separated," she says softly. "My dad moved out to a flat in Granville. I'm still at home with Mum but I'll have to decide who I want to live with permanently. . . My family has collapsed. . ."

Her chin starts to quiver and I jump up and hug her tightly, feeling thoroughly ashamed of myself. I hold her for ages, letting her cry against my shoulder. I let her tell me about slammed doors and TV dinners. Sleeping tablets and silence so loud it deafens. How her father and mother fell out of love and into hate. That there were days she stared at the shadows on her walls, feeling utterly alone. That there were times she resented me for not forcing her to talk; for not being there. And suddenly I realize that true friends are those who love you not in spite of your faults and imperfections, but because of them.

45

"So have you got a date?" Peter asks Paul loudly as we wait for the teacher to arrive. "Or couldn't you find anybody who'd accept payment?"

"Shut it, Peter," Paul says. "You think you're funny but you put me to sleep."

The rest of the class gets caught up in the excitement of a confrontation and turns to watch Peter in action.

"Oooh, is that the best you've got?" Peter taunts. "Why don't you ask Tina from applied maths? Fat chicks will take anybody."

He high-fives Sam and they collapse over their egos. Timothy walks into class and their radar shifts.

"Who are you taking, Goldfish?" Peter asks. "I don't

think even a fat chick would lower her standards for you."

"Really?" he says. "Then why did your mum say yes?" The class erupts into laughter and Peter looks furious.

"You piece of shit. Don't even go there."

"I don't like going to a lot of places, Peter, but you're the one handing out the invitations."

Some of us stare in awe at Timothy. Hardly anybody has the ability to rile Peter the way Timothy does.

"Come up close and say it to my face, you chicken shit," Peter says.

"Your bum cheeks aren't the ideal exposure for my complexion."

I stare at Timothy and I feel proud. Proud to know him. Lucky to have befriended him. Ashamed to have doubted him. This is a guy with spunk. His confidence doesn't come at the expense of others, in the way it does with Peter. It lights up from within. He's taught me to only give a damn about people that matter.

He's one of those people. He's one of my best friends. And I'm going to get him back.

Miss Sajda is at our house for coffee tonight. We spend time discussing how we can get Dad out of the musk habit and into a department store aftershave counter. My dad is refusing to budge and changes the topic to their wedding plans.

It's going to be a low-key affair in a couple of months'

time. They're hiring a marquee in our backyard and inviting about fifty or so family friends. As we're discussing the flower arrangements, Bilal walks into the living room, the telephone in his hand.

"That was Amy," he tells me. I reach over to grab the telephone from him but he pulls it back. "I told her you'll call her back."

"Why?"

He silences me with his eyes and asks me to make him a cup of tea.

"Make it yourself," I say.

"Just make it, *please*," he says through gritted teeth. There's a lot of funny eyeball action going on and I don't have the faintest clue what messages he's trying to send me so I get up in a huff and go into the kitchen.

I can only assume that he's got something private to discuss with my dad and Miss Sajda so I naturally press my ear to the kitchen door and try my best to decipher what they're saying.

"Her formal is on this Friday, Dad," Bilal says.

My heart stops.

"Is it?" my dad asks, not sounding particularly interested.

"Her whole class is going."

I'm pretty sure I hear my dad sigh. He smokes a packet of cigarettes a day so any lung activity is usually shared with the entire street.

"We've been through this before."

"I'll take her," Bilal says.

AGH!

Double AGH!

"Nothing can happen if she's with me. I'll be with her all night and I'll drop her off home. OK, Dad?"

"It sounds fair, Hakim," Miss Sajda says. "I don't want to interfere with how you raise your children —"

No, please do!

"— but if Bilal takes her you should have nothing to worry about."

I positively love my stepmother-to-be.

"Did she set this up?" my dad asks.

"I swear to God she didn't, Dad," Bilal says. "It's my idea."

"Since when are you so kind to your sister?"

I hear Bilal laugh. "I just feel sorry for her. Her friend was on the phone now. She wanted to know if we'd be home on Friday night because she planned on getting flowers delivered to Jamilah."

"*Flowers?*"

"Yeah, because she feels bad that Jamilah's not going."

My dad lets out a snort of laughter. "Are you serious?"

"Yeah! And I thought how unbelievably sad and pathetic. Jamilah's not some sick kid."

"What a sweet friend," my dad says. "How do I know I can trust you, Bilal? You won't drop her off and go out? You will stay with her the whole night?"

"I promise I'll stay with her, Dad. You have my word."

Inhale. Exhale. Exhale. Exhale. No, inhale more. You need an inhale!

There is a long, excruciating pause. Like somebody slowly peeling a band-aid off a wound.

And then it finally comes off.

"OK."

There are miracles and there are MIRACLES.

Lower-case miracles are things like green traffic lights all the way to the airport when you're running late for a flight. Getting an A+ on an exam you haven't studied for. Finding a one hundred dollar note in a box of bran flakes (that's never happened to me but it fits the category).

Upper-case miracles are things like car crash survival stories. The successful separation of Siamese twins.

And my dad granting me permission to go to the formal.

"AGHHHHH!" I cry, unceremoniously falling through the kitchen door and into the living room. I jump on to my dad and smother him in kisses. Then I leap on to Bilal and smother him in kisses. And then Miss Sajda. And then back to my dad.

Miss Sajda and my dad are doubled over in laughter and Bilal wipes his sleeve across his face.

"Sheez, save it for Dad, will you?" he says, a disgusted look on his face.

"You're the best!" I cry.

"Yeah, well, nothing comes for free. You're ironing my shirts for a month."

"A *month*!"

"I can always be at Cave nightclub on Friday night instead, you know."

"No nightclubs!" my dad cries.

"But a *month*?"

"It's funk night too." He starts singing one of his favourite songs.

"Bilal! Do not swear in this house!" my dad yells.

Miss Sajda, Bilal and I look at each other and burst into a fit of giggles.

"F–U–N–K," Bilal says slowly and clearly.

My dad looks at Miss Sajda, shakes his head and lifts his hands in the air as if to say "kids nowadays". They fall into that lovey-dovey "we're so in love and share the same sense of humour" laughter. That's my cue to bounce off to my bedroom and spend the rest of the evening on the telephone with Amy, discussing how I'm to find a dress, hairdresser and make-up stylist in four days.

46

The dress can't be sleeveless, short, transparent, slinky, low-cut or too revealing.

"So basically I've got two options!" I tell my dad, my hands on my hips, my nostrils flaring. "A pair of pyjamas or a full-length leotard!"

"Just as long as the leotard isn't too figure-hugging," he says, grinning.

I let out a frustrated wail and throw myself on to the couch. I frown. I glare. I pout. My father is unmoved.

"You are only achieving premature ageing, darling," he says.

"Oh Hakim, don't be such a tease," Miss Sajda scolds. She's at our house for dinner tonight.

It's seven twenty on Wednesday evening. I have twenty-eight hours and forty minutes until the formal. That's not a lot of time. Especially when all I have planned is a home appointment with a hairdresser (one of Shereen's university friends who used to work in a salon but quit to study political science) and a make-up artist (me).

Tomorrow night is my only hope. It will be late-night shopping and if I don't find a dress I will have no choice but to show up in my school uniform with a flower stuck on the collar for special effect.

I search the internet for all the latest catalogues at my favourite shops. It is impossible to find anything that fits Dad's description of modest. I storm back into the lounge room.

"Does a potato sack attached to a king-size quilt satisfy your criteria?"

"Maybe," he says. He doesn't bother looking up from his newspaper.

"*Dad!*"

"You can get away with a sleeveless dress if you can find a nice shawl to drape over your shoulders."

I turn around, startled by Miss Sajda's voice. My father slowly looks up from his newspaper. "I don't want her wearing sleeveless."

"Hakim, nothing will show. A shawl solves the problem with most of the formal dresses out there. In fact, a lot of the shops sell shawls on the side, so it would just be a matter of finding a colour and fabric to match. If we can't, we can always buy some fabric and I can use an overlocker over the edges."

I look at my dad hopefully. He clears his throat. Tugs at his collar. He doesn't respond but sits quietly, listening to Miss Sajda.

"If the dress is too low-cut, we can always pin the shawl in such a way that it covers Jamilah's chest. We'll just need to get a double layer of the material."

"So her shoulders will be covered?"

"Oh yes, definitely. Don't worry, Hakim!" she says in a reassuring voice when she notices the worried look on his face. "Leave female fashion to me."

He pauses. My neck prickles in anticipation. Finally he responds. "Fine," he says gruffly.

"Yippee!" I squeal in delight.

"Can you . . . take Jamilah to the shops tomorrow and help her?"

I give Miss Sajda an imploring smile.

"I'd be happy to. Is that OK with you, Jamilah?"

"Of course!"

She beams happily at me. "How about I find a new pair of shoes for you too, Hakim? Maybe without masseur soles?"

He leans back in his chair and stretches his legs out, his tan-coloured slippers poking out. "Stick with shawls," he says, a grin on his face. "The masseur soles are staying."

Miss Sajda turns to me and winks. "That's what he thinks," she whispers and we burst out laughing.

286

47

The dress is different shades of lime and turquoise and teal. It's long and elegant. It's sleeveless but it isn't low-cut and snuggles comfortably against my body. I found a matching shawl and Miss Sajda has draped it over my shoulders and around my arms, just above my elbows. She's pinned it to the edges of my dress so that it won't slip.

I'm sitting stiff and rigid in my dress on a chair in front of my bedroom mirror, careful to avoid any sudden or violent movements in case the pins come undone. Shereen's friend, Talia, is styling my hair.

When Talia walked into the house I nearly dropped dead. Her hair is dyed pink; the sides are shaved with only a short ponytail left dangling from the back. I took one look at her and dragged Shereen to another room, demanding to know if this was her idea of a sick joke.

She was unaffected by my hyperventilating state. A cool and calm "Trust me" was all she could offer.

Because I only had one hour until Bilal picked me up in his friend's silver BMW I had no choice but to take her advice.

In a mere twenty-five minutes Talia demolishes my stereotypes about the hairdressing abilities of someone with a pink-ponytailed shaved head and produces a hairstyle that belongs on a Paris catwalk.

"Wow! Thanks," I gush, admiring her handiwork in the mirror.

"Do you need help with your make-up?" she asks.

I guess I haven't matured that much because I take one look at her blue eyeshadow on one eye and green eyeshadow on the other and decline her offer.

I go into the bathroom, spread my make-up supplies across the benchtop, throw a towel across my chest like a bib to prevent any make-up from falling on to my dress, and start applying. I'm so nervous about getting my make-up just right that my hands aren't very steady and I'm in danger of making a complete mess of my face. I'm negotiating a mascara wand when Miss Sajda knocks on the door and offers to lend me a helping hand.

Because I'm nervous, and because I have to admit that as out of touch with her birth certificate as she may be, Miss

Sajda can do wicked things with an eyeshadow wand, I accept.

And so here I am standing in my bathroom on a Friday night. I'm getting ready for my Year Ten formal. I'm taking my older brother as my personal bodyguard. I'm being made up by my dad's new fiancée, who just happens to be my madrasa teacher. And to top it all off, there will be no sunset rule tonight and there isn't an "I'm studying at Amy's" excuse in sight.

If you'd told me to predict this scene several months ago I would have laughed in your face. It sure is starting to feel a little surreal.

Miss Sajda does an amazing job. Sure, she subjects me to a long story about the history of black eyeliner (*kohl* powder in Arabic) in the Middle East but I can't complain. She's given me extra-volume lashes that curl. Knowing that kohl was once believed to have value as a protection against eye disease is a small price to pay.

After being made up and blow-waved and pinned and hairsprayed and perfumed and lipstick-on-my-teeth checked, I walk out into the living room where my dad and Bilal are sitting. I'm carrying my *darabuka* with me.

My dad looks closely at my outfit, scrutinizing it as I move about the living room.

"Well? Does it meet your approval, caveman?" I say to him, standing over him with my hands folded across my chest.

"*Caveman?*"

"Yep!"

He looks over at Miss Sajda and rolls his eyes, trying to disguise a grin. "See how she treats her father?" he asks in a mock mortified tone. "This is the gratitude I get for letting her go to a place where they will dance to shameless music and she will return corrupted—"

"Yeah OK, Dad," Bilal interrupts impatiently, "we get it. We're running late because Jamilah thinks she's going to meet royalty and has taken bloody hours to get ready!"

I ignore the quip (he's just saved me from a lecture) and we all walk outside to the BMW. Shereen has her camera and is taking photos of me as though I were a bride leaving home on her wedding day.

My dad sees the number plate and nearly passes out on the driveway.

SEXY4U.

"Eh! Bilal! What is this rubbish?"

Bilal grits his teeth. "It's my friend's car, Dad. Relax."

Miss Sajda is in the background, stifling a laugh.

"I don't like it! How can Jamilah go in a car with that kind of immoral number plate?"

"Dad!" I groan. "No one's going to think anything."

"What if somebody we know sees you?"

I burst out laughing. "Ha! They'll think Bilal's sexy for them!"

My dad isn't amused and I see his eyes dart over to his taxi and a familiar expression of contemplation shadow his face.

Anticipating his thoughts I lash out. "No way! Absolutely not! I am NOT going to my formal in your TAXI!"

Bilal throws his head in his hands. Shereen cries out to Dad to lighten up. Miss Sajda steps close to Dad and talks to him. I can't hear what she's saying but whatever it is I want her to keep going because the "I'm about to go into cardiac arrest" expression on his face is slowly subsiding.

He waves his hand and we know that we've won.

Who needs a cardiovascular workout when you live with my dad? My heart gets more pumped up in an hour with him than it would in a high-impact aerobics class.

I kiss him goodbye and I notice that he is almost teary. "You look beautiful, Jamilah," he says.

I swear my dad is going through the male version of menopause. Hot flushes over number plates and two-second mood swings. We need pharmaceutical attention here.

"Be good, don't take the shawl off and stay close to Bilal."

"Yes, Dad."

We zoom off.

We pull up into the car park of the reception hall at seven thirty. It's a spectacularly grand building, cement-rendered white, with two large pillars at the entrance and red carpet laid up the front steps that lead into the double stained-glass doors. Lining the steps are lush green hedges shaped like lollipops that jut out of tall terracotta vases.

We wait behind the queue of cars lined up in search of a

parking space, and I break out into a small sweat as I observe groups of students walking with their dates through the car park towards the entrance. Other couples and groups are hanging around a large fountain in front of the entrance steps, laughing and joking with each other.

Most of the guys are transformed beings in their crisp suits and polished shoes. There are those out to make a different kind of statement. Some wear runners under their suits; others wear T-shirts under their jackets (Eminem and 2-Pac both make an appearance). One guy, who is dressed in a black suit, has opted for the Ronald McDonald look with a bright red wig and red shoes.

But it's the girls who steal the show tonight, with their dresses in assorted colours and designs, and their elaborate hairstyles and glittering jewellery.

"Are you going to hang out with me all night?" I ask Bilal after we've found a car space and are making our way to the entrance.

"Dad's orders," he answers in a deadpan voice.

I grab his arm anxiously. "Really?"

His mouth twitches.

"Ha!" I cry. "You're joking, right?"

He grins. "What do you think? Just have your fun and stop worrying."

I nudge him in the side and smile gratefully at him.

"Anyway, you're lucky I'm so good-looking," he says, giving me a wink. "Trust me. Being seen with me does wonders for the rep."

I make a retching noise and he advises me that I'm making my lipstick look lopsided so I stop.

To my dismay, Bilal's older-brother conceit may be justified for once. As we join a group of my classmates I notice the girls' mouths drop in awe as they look Bilal up and down. They mill around me, whispering questions into my ear.

"Who's the hunk?"

"How old is he?"

"Where'd you pick *him* up from?!"

I feel my head swell with pride as I tell them he's my brother. They're impressed. Bilal has come into use and I can't stop beaming.

I catch sight of Amy and her date, Lindsay. I rush over to her and we head to the dance floor. Lindsay makes us laugh as he clowns around to some of the songs. Bilal is at our table eating my pasta entrée. I'm having too much of a good time to even think about food. A couple of girls are sitting next to him, flirting and trying to get him to notice them. His head is expanding at an exponential rate.

"You look distracted," Amy says.

"Have you seen Timothy?"

"No, I haven't."

We continue dancing until I break off to look for Timothy. I'm walking past the bar when I notice Peter, Sam and Liz huddled together. I'm not in the mood for speaking to them but it's too late. They've spotted me.

"The music sucks," Peter sneers. "They must have hired a try-hard DJ."

"It's not that bad," I say. "Actually it sounds fine to me."

Liz is snuggled into Sam's arms and refuses to meet my gaze.

"So where's your date?" Peter asks.

"Around." I look away from his prying eyes and self-consciously play with the edge of my shawl.

"Hmm. . . So did you borrow your outfit from a nun?" I should have known that he wouldn't take rejection easily. "I'm just kidding. You look great. Really you do. Lots of fabric works wonders."

I gulp hard, cutting my fingernails into the palms of my hands. I look at Liz but she turns her face away. "That's not very nice," I say.

"I was wrong about you. I don't think you have a wild side. Or any *secrets*. I think you're just. . ." He taps his finger on his chin and looks up, a contemplative expression on his face. "What's the word. . .? Ah, yes. Boring. Plain old *boring*."

Sam bursts out laughing and I turn on my heels and walk off, struggling to control my quivering chin. I storm up to my table and tap on Bilal's shoulder.

"I want to go," I say. "Take me home."

He drops his spoon on to the table and stands up, taking my hand in his. "Why? What's wrong? Did somebody hurt you? I'll smash their face!"

I choke back tears and he leads me away to a quiet corner.

"What happened?"

I take a deep breath and lean back against the wall. "Have you seen Timothy?"

"Timothy? You mean the guy with the lawyer mum?"

I nod and he shakes his head. "Why? Do you want me to smash him?"

"*Bilal!* I don't want you to *smash* anybody."

"But you've been crying. It's your night, Jam. You're supposed to be happy. I'm missing out on a funk night, remember?"

He gives me an affectionate look and I smile. "I don't think I can go through with it, Bilal. I don't think I can play in the band."

"Then don't," he says casually. "It's no big deal."

But it is. He doesn't know how much it means to me.

"Oh Bilal. You don't understand."

"Wait there, one second. OK?"

I nod and he dashes off. I'm rubbing smudged make-up from the bottom of my eyelids when he returns. I turn around and Timothy is there, standing tall and graceful in a black tux.

"She's been looking for you," Bilal says. "Apparently I don't understand. I'm guessing you do. Hurt her, and I'll smash you. Be nice to her and you can come and chill with me. I've got an extra plate of pasta if you're still hungry." He winks at me and walks away.

"What's going on?" He gives me a confused look.

I smile self-consciously. "Forget it. Anyway, where have you been? I've been looking for you."

"I made friends with the DJ."

"I owe you an apology."

"You owe me an apology for not accepting my apology. There, we're even."

I laugh out loud in surprise. "That was easy. I had a whole speech planned."

"I can understand why you were initially angry. It would have come as a shock to you. It did to me when I realized I was emailing you."

"I've thought long and hard about it. And you didn't take advantage of me. You blocked me pretty soon after you found out. Boy was I pissed off with you!"

He laughs. "Why?"

"Because *John* was the first person I'd ever opened up to. But then we started getting closer and it felt so familiar and comfortable. I didn't miss John as much any more."

"Can I ask you something?"

"Yeah."

"Who am I talking to? Jamilah or Jamie?"

I smile and look into his eyes. "Jamie's gone, Timothy."

He suddenly steps forward, grabs both of my hands and kisses me on the lips. Then he leans back, still holding my hands tightly in his.

I'm stunned. It feels like an electric shock. Like every cell in my body is on fire with the excitement of it. I feel like jumping up and down with delight. I feel like laughing. He makes me feel like a salty summer breeze. Like a sail boat bobbing up and down on the harbour under a cloudless day.

But then, out of the corner of my eye, I catch Bilal looking our way from across the room. I can tell by the expression on his face that he hadn't seen Timothy kiss me. But his face is scrunched up with confusion, having seen me so close to Timothy. He stretches tall on the tip of his toes and tries to get a closer look.

I quickly drop my hands and step back, keeping my distance from Timothy. I wave at Bilal, trying to disguise the guilty expression on my face. He slowly waves back and then turns around.

"I can't do this," I whisper to myself.

"What? I can't hear you."

I look up at Timothy and give him a gentle smile. "I'm sorry, Timothy. But I can't do this."

"What do you mean?"

"This. *Us*. I can't do it at this point. The timing is all wrong."

"Why?"

I sigh and fumble anxiously with my hands. "For the first time in my life I've decided to be honest. With myself, with my friends, with my family. To be with you would mean I'd have to go behind my dad's back. I've just discovered honesty and trust. And for once in my life I have a relationship with my dad. I don't want to lose that."

He stares down at the floor. Then up at the ceiling. Then back at the floor. He sighs heavily.

"There's no chance he'd come round?"

I chuckle. "Not in a million years. I care for you, Timothy. A lot. But I also care about keeping the peace between Dad and me. I'm through with the lies and deceit."

This is what I love about Timothy. He understands me. He gives me space when I need it. He doesn't take crap from me. I've talked to him, I've read him, and it's been like fish and chips in butcher's paper and fizzy lemonade in a glass bottle. All I want is for us to forget John and Jamie and start over as Timothy and Jamilah. But as best friends. This is my first test. And if being with Timothy means deceiving my father, then I'm willing to put that desire aside. It hurts to reject Timothy. Choosing honesty isn't always easy. I just know it's the right thing to do.

He takes a deep breath. "Oh boy," he says, exhaling heavily and running his fingers through his hair. "Well, I can't very well resent you for wanting to do the whole *true to myself* thing. Not after all we've been through."

His smile is warm and sincere and it almost makes me want to cry.

"You're special, Timothy."

"You're breaking my heart here, Jamilah," he says, trying to sound cheerful as he shakes his head.

I lean over and gently place my hand on his arm. "Thanks for everything."

There's no need for words. We walk back to our table, enjoying the comfortable silence between friends.

Mustafa storms up to me and grabs me by the arm. I'm sitting with Timothy, Bilal, Amy and Lindsay. We're eating our main course, listening to Bilal's stories.

"Here you are! Man, come on backstage! We have to go

through some pre-performance logistics! I'll see you there in five. You dig?"

"Yeah, I dig," I say and he gives me the peace sign and hurries away.

Mr Anderson gets up on to the stage and makes an announcement that the band will be performing in fifteen minutes. Anybody wanting to dance along to the performance is invited to the dance floor.

Peter is sitting at a nearby table. He makes a loud booing noise. Bilal looks behind and then back at me, rolling his eyes in Peter's direction.

We all stand up. Everybody wants a good position on the dance floor. We head down, crossing paths with Peter, Chris, Sam and Liz as we do. They have no problem sharing their lack of enthusiasm.

"What a frigging joke!" Peter cries. "Now we have to put up with these bloody wogs and their desert music."

Bilal's eyes turn into slits, as narrow as two coin slots. I gently place my hand on his arm and shake my head.

Peter is oblivious. "I mean, this is *Australia* not bloody Iraq."

"That's it," Bilal says, pushing my arm away and tapping Peter on the shoulder. We all stop to watch.

"Do you want to shut your trap or do you want me to do it for you?"

"Who the hell do you think. . .?" Peter's voice trails off as he turns around and notices Bilal's size. "What's your problem?" he asks, his voice slightly shaky.

"My problem is that you're a racist dickhead. I've just eaten two bowls of pasta. I'm on carb overload here, so connecting your face to the floor isn't really going to take much effort. My sister's playing in that *wog* band. She's going to kick arse. And I'm going to kick yours if you don't shove that tongue back down into that miserable throat of yours. Do you understand?"

Peter shrivels up. He looks over at me in astonishment and I fold my arms across my chest and stare back at him, daring him to say something. He looks back at Bilal, who's towering over him, gives a feeble sneer and, quickly walks away. We all stare in awe at Bilal and let out a whooping cheer.

I hitch the bag containing my *darabuka* under my arm. Bilal gives me a quick hug. Timothy winks at me. Amy squeezes my hand. I smile at them and walk backstage. I know that I'll never feel alone again.

Mustafa, Samira and Hasan are anxiously waiting for me.

"The concert starts in ten minutes," Samira cries. "We're on soon! Are you all ready?"

"Yep!" I pat my bag and she smiles with relief.

I make a quick trip to the toilets. I lean over a basin and put some water on my cheeks, careful not to ruin my make-up. I take in deep breaths, shaking my hands about and looking at myself in the mirror.

"You can do this," I whisper to myself. I stare long and hard at my reflection but I slowly start to look distorted and lopsided and it freaks me out so I stare at the bath tiles instead.

The schizophrenia sets in about three seconds later.

Voice 1 (A mix of Timothy and Amy): Don't panic. You have nothing to be ashamed of. It's your heritage. It's cool. You know the *darabuka* is awesome. They'll love it.

Voice 2 (Jamie loud and clear): Don't be such an idiot. How daggy can you get? The *darabuka*? At your Year Ten formal? Run while you still have a chance to save your dignity. It's WOGGY beyond belief. You will never live it down. They'll know you're Arabic! And then what? Do you seriously want to open up the way for all the tea-towel and terrorist and camel-jockey jokes? Sprint!

Voice 3 (Aunt Sowsan): You should have eaten some of the pasta. Solids in the stomach would have helped you cope. Although the pasta did look a little too creamy. That could have been dangerous too.

Voice 4 (Miss Sajda): Darling, *habibi*, don't concern yourself with the creamy pasta. Years of garlic sauce on kebabs have given you a great constitution. Just have your fun! Be proud of who you are! Remove the disguise. And step out of the world of anonymity.

And so that's what I decide to do.

I return to my group and stand behind the curtain waiting for Mr Anderson to finish introducing us. The crowd claps and cheers and we step out on to the stage. The internal karate moves don't stop but I try my best to ignore them, looking out into the sea of faces and bodies. I see Amy and Timothy and they wave wildly at me. Bilal is standing to the side of the dance floor, hands folded across his chest, chest pumped up, thoroughly enjoying the attention of the girls who are buzzing around him. We make eye contact and he gives me the thumbs-up.

We each take our individual positions on the stage and set up our instruments. I place the *darabuka* under my arm and crack my knuckles.

This is it. I gulp hard.

Mustafa, not content with Mr Anderson's welcome preamble, grabs the microphone, adopts his "I'm a sick bro in the hood" attitude, and proceeds to get the crowd in even more of a whirl.

"Yo! Whassup y'all? We're gonna FREAK tonight! This group behind me here is the bling of tonight's formal!"

The crowd cheers. One person yells out, "Get on with it, ya P.Diddy wannabe!"

"Tonight is about Aussie-Ethnic pride! We're the OzWogs! And we're gonna make you shake your arses!"

The crowd hears Mustafa say "arses" and starts cheering. I look over at Mr Anderson. He looks aghast.

"Let's get the party STARTED y'all!"

My God, I think to myself, does Mustafa need a Macquarie English dictionary or what?

The stage lights dim and Mustafa and Hasan start on their keyboards, sounding out a stream of dance and techno beats that *doof doof* through our bodies. The beats start slow and then start to intensify, getting faster and wilder. On my cue, I start striking the centre and edges of the *darabuka* with the palms of my hands. The music drums out and reverberates into the night as the stage floor microphones pick up the beats. I look out at a sea of faces. Most people are in awe. We've combined techno and dance, Eastern with Western, and the crowd is loving it. Suddenly Hayaat, a Lebanese girl; Stella, a Greek girl; and Caroline, an Anglo girl, jump up on to the stage and start dancing to the music, shifting between hip-hop, funk and belly-dancing shakes of their hips and torsos. As the music intensifies, their moves become faster and they flirt with the air, swinging their hips, swaying their arms and kicking their legs. The crowd responds with frenzied cheers.

I spot Peter, Chris and Sam. They're huddled together, scowls on their faces. Liz is looking up in surprise. I grin down at them.

We keep on playing and the *darabuka* picks me up from my chair and lifts me into another dimension. I'm floating above the crowd, watching them celebrate my music, drinking it up like chilled strawberry cordial on a summer's day.

I can't believe I'm here, at my formal, in front of all my classmates, exposing myself like this. There's no shame; there's no embarrassment. With every drumming down on the *darabuka* I'm announcing who I am. For the first time in my life, knowing the answer has never felt so sweet.

Look out for…

Does
My
Head
Look
Big
In
This?

…the brilliant first novel
by Randa Abdel-Fattah

**High school is tough enough without
throwing a hijab into the mix…**

15-year-old Amal's decision to wear the Muslim
veil full-time takes a lot of guts. Can she cope
with the prejudice, keep her friends, and still
attract the cutest boy in school?

"Every teenager in the UK should read this book"
Sunday Times

MARION LLOYD BOOKS

Look out for...

BEAST

by

ALLY KENNEN

Stephen is a boy with a dangerous secret. For four years
he has kept a terrifying creature locked up in a remote
hiding place. Once just a vicious little baby, it is now a
powerful predator, big and hungry enough to break free
from its rusting cage...

"I really love this book ... *Beast* should be a monster hit"
The Times

Shortlisted for the Booktrust Teenage Prize

MARION LLOYD BOOKS

Look out for...

BERSERK

by

ALLY KENNEN

Sometimes trouble just runs in the family...

Stephen may have dealt with the BEAST – but for his
15-year-old brother Chas, things are just getting
started. When he comes across a website asking
people to be pen pals with prisoners on Death Row,
he writes to an inmate, because he thinks it will be
funny to get letters from a murderer.
The chilling replies are not at all what he expects,
and what follows is terrifyingly close to home...

mlb

MARION LLOYD BOOKS

Don't miss

Life as we knew it

by

Susan Pfeffer

No shops. No TV.

No electricity. No daylight.

No idea if your family
is alive or dead...

Could *you* survive?

An asteroid will hit the moon at 9.30
this evening. The astronomers say
there's nothing to worry about.

What if they're wrong?

*Susan Pfeffer's thrilling story of a catastrophic
natural disaster catapults you into a terrifyingly real
world – where life as we know it has gone for ever.*

MARION LLOYD BOOKS

DATE DUE
